Secret Identities and Double Lives on Tween TV

Secret Identities and Double Lives on Tween TV introduces readers to the concepts of tweenhood and television (TV) tropes by providing historical and theoretical contexts and reviewing the history of TV targeted to tweens.

Through a qualitative analysis of various live-action sitcoms, this book explores the popularity of programming featuring characters leading secret lives and targeted to tweens. By unpacking various theoretical explanations of this distinct period of life and examining them through the critical lens of the content of these tween TV shows that feature secret identities, the book offers a unique understanding of the tween experience woven in the nexus of power, morality, friendship, romance, family life, and self-identity.

This book's analysis and understanding would benefit children's media scholars and researchers, students of media studies, communication studies, cultural studies, adolescent studies, and child development.

Amy Richards Franzini is Professor of Communication Studies at Widener University, USA. She studies the representations of children, childhood, parents, and parenting in popular media. She has written chapters in the books *Fleeting Images: Portrayals of Children in Popular Culture* and *Common Sense: Intelligence as Presented on Popular Television,* and has articles published in *Journal of Sex Research, Communication Teacher* and *Journal of Children and Media.*

Routledge Focus on Television Studies

The Evolution of Black Women in Television
Mammies, Matriarchs and Mistresses
Imani M. Cheers

Heroism, Celebrity and Therapy in Nurse Jackie
Christopher Pullen

Re-scheduling Television in the Digital Era
Hanne Bruun

Digital Food TV
The Cultural Place of Food in a Digital Era
Michelle Phillipov

TV Shows and Nonplace
Why *The Sopranos*, *Breaking Bad* and Co. Love the Periphery
Alexander Gutzmer

Adam West as a Signature Role TV Star
Carl Sweeney

Social Media Television and Distributional Aesthetics
Gry C. Rustad

The Intersectional Athlete Body on Reality TV
MTV's The Challenge
Laura Langalde

Secret Identities and Double Lives on Tween TV
Amy Richards Franzini

Secret Identities and Double Lives on Tween TV

Amy Richards Franzini

LONDON AND NEW YORK

First published 2025
by Routledge
4 Park Square, Milton Park, Abingdon, Oxon OX14 4RN

and by Routledge
605 Third Avenue, New York, NY 10158

Routledge is an imprint of the Taylor & Francis Group, an informa business

British Library Cataloguing-in-Publication Data
A catalogue record for this book is available from the British Library

Library of Congress Cataloging-in-Publication Data
Names: Franzini, Amy Richards, author.
Title: Secret identities and double lives on tween TV / Amy Richards Franzini.
Description: London ; New York : Routledge, 2025. | Series: Routledge focus on television studies | Includes bibliographical references and index.
Identifiers: LCCN 2024061991 (print) | LCCN 2024061992 (ebook) | ISBN 9781032972695 (hardback) | ISBN 9781032972701 (paperback) | ISBN 9781003593027 (ebook)
Subjects: LCSH: Teen television programs--United States--History and criticism. | Situation comedies (Television programs)--United States--History and criticism. | Youth on television. | Identity (Psychology) on television.
Classification: LCC PN1992.8.Y68 F73 2025 (print) | LCC PN1992.8.Y68 (ebook) | DDC 384.55/506573--dc23/eng/20250205
LC record available at https://lccn.loc.gov/2024061991
LC ebook record available at https://lccn.loc.gov/2024061992

ISBN: 978-1-032-97269-5 (hbk)
ISBN: 978-1-032-97270-1 (pbk)
ISBN: 978-1-003-59302-7 (ebk)

DOI: 10.4324/9781003593027

Typeset in Times New Roman
by SPi Technologies India Pvt Ltd (Straive)

To Jake, Max, and Kate.
Thank you for introducing me to many of these programs.
I love that my research involved spending time with you.

Contents

Acknowledgments

Since this is a book about double lives, I need to thank people in both of my lives – my professional life and my personal life. In my professional life I'd like to thank my colleagues, students, and friends at Widener University in Chester, PA. I'd especially like to thank Dr. Angie Corbo, Dr. Timothy Scepansky, and Dr. Jennifer Reinwald of Widener's Communication Studies Department for their unwavering support.

In my personal life, I am grateful to my friends and family for encouragement as I worked on this project. My biggest thanks belong to my husband, Steve, and my children Jake, Max, and Kate for their patience and grace as I completed this book.

1 Introduction

It is mind-boggling to imagine how much TV viewing has changed for tweens since TVs were introduced into American homes in the 1950s. In the early 1960s a 10-year-old child would likely watch programs such as *The Andy Griffith Show* or *The Beverly Hillbillies* weekly with their parents. If they missed a program the night it was on, they were out-of-luck; but it was unlikely they would miss it because this was a way of spending time as a family.

These programs were being broadcast in the truest sense of the word – targeting the broadest audience possible, both young and old. Jump ahead just 20 short years and cable TV was on the rise, with two cable channels specifically targeting children: Nickelodeon and Disney Channel. Now shows were being specifically aimed at children, though still a bit broadly, to children of all ages and backgrounds. Even so, traditional network TV was still producing shows that were meant to be consumed by the entire family: case in point ABC's TGIF programming block in the 1990s.

As cable TV continued to grow into the 2000s, audience segmentation became even narrower, with children's TV dividing further to target preschool children, school-aged children, and teenagers. The popularization of smartphones in the 2010s together with the rapid growth of streaming has totally reimagined TV viewing for young people. A 10-year-old child today can watch hundreds of programs targeted directly to kids similar to them in age and/or interests. Children can watch these programs on an actual TV, a tablet, a computer, or a smartphone. They can watch one episode, or they can binge-watch an entire season or more of most programs – even shows their parents watched when *they* were young.

Given this revolution in children's TV, it is both interesting and important to explore programming that is produced specifically for children and tweens. By examining themes and tropes that are popular in shows targeting this demographic, we can gain insight not only into these programs, but into the children that view them as well. This book seeks to explore one specific type of programming: live-action sitcoms featuring young

DOI: 10.4324/9781003593027-1

adolescent characters. Even more specifically, this book will delve into a popular trope for these sitcoms: secret identities and double lives. Why have there been so many live-action sitcoms that feature characters who lead secret lives? And why might they be particularly popular with the tween audience?

The second chapter of this book will review the history of tween TV and discuss the uniqueness of the tween audience. Relevant developmental psychology and media theories will be used to explain why these specific types of programs might be attractive to this specialized audience. Of particular importance will be theories of self-identity, including the concept of "possible selves." Tweens are not quite teens, but these programs can provide a sitcom-stylized view of what teenagerhood might hold for them in the future.

Once we've laid a foundation as to who is watching these programs, the third chapter will examine the genre of live-action sitcoms targeting tweens generally and the trope of secret identities and double lives more specifically. Why do stories of pop stars, witches, wizards, spies, and superheroes resonate particularly to tweens?

In the remaining chapters, connections between tweens' self-identity and themes related to the secret-identity-trope will be fleshed out. In each chapter the theoretical underpinnings of the chapters' foci will first be reviewed and then examples from the secret-identity tween sitcoms will be shared.

Tweenhood is a time of life when autonomy is blossoming but not able to be fully tested. However, these programs showcase young characters whose secret identities allow them to wield power. Power will be explored in Chapter 4 in overt and obvious ways – through superhero, witch, or wizarding power – and in more subtle ways, like the power of choosing to either reveal or keep one's secret identity, secret.

Next, Chapter 5 will explore themes relating to finding one's moral compass. This is most obviously played out in the superhero programs such as *Mighty Med*, *Henry Danger*, *The Thundermans*, and *The Villains of Valley View*, where there are regular battles between good and evil. But more subtle examples of characters finding their moral compass can be seen not just in the "secret identity" portion of their lives, but carried over into their "regular-everyday-lives" as well. Many of these characters need to exercise control and follow specific rules to keep their identities secret. Still, they test the limits and sometimes suffer repercussions as a result.

Besides identity exploration, another area of adolescence that is highlighted in these programs is relationship formation and maintenance. Relationships with friends, romantic relationships, and family relationships are all explored in these programs. As with the identity themes, these relational themes being played out allow tweens to explore potential relational issues before they happen to them in their own lives.

Friendship is a key storytelling device in live-action sitcoms targeting tweens, and will be discussed in Chapter 6. In a few of the programs, lead characters are friends, like in *Mighty Med* and *The Villains of Valley View*, while in most of the others the lead characters decide early on whether or not to reveal their secret identities to their friends. The chapter on friendship will explore this further.

Romantic relationships are explored in most of these secret-identity tween programs and will be explored in Chapter 7. Just as with friendships, the choice to reveal a character's secret identity to their love interest plays a major role in these stories. Issues of trust and fear of rejection are both motivations that are investigated through these choices. In some programs, the additional weight of dating someone dissimilar is discussed, such as Alex (a wizard) dating Mason, a werewolf, in *Wizards of Waverly Place*.

Besides friendships and romances, most themes on these programs revolve around family, and as such, the book features three chapters that are family-focused. First, Chapter 8 explores sibling relationships, then Chapter 9 focuses on characters' relationships with parents and guardians. In some programs the protagonist's parents are not aware of their secret identities, such as *Henry Danger*, and *Ultra-Violet & Black Scorpion*. How do relationships differ in these cases? Sibling rivalry is a key storytelling element of a number of these programs, such as *K.C. Undercover*, *The Thundermans*, and *Wizards of Waverly Place*. Both *The Thundermans* and *Wizards of Waverly Place* feature explicit storylines that allow only one sibling to retain their special powers. This exaggerates already tense sibling relationships and provides space for the concept of family loyalty to be investigated. Relationships with extended family members, such as cousins and grandparents, will also be discussed in Chapter 10. Chapter 10 will also address the mentorship of characters by non-family members.

Finally, the closing chapter of the book will explore if and how these characters ultimately decide to reveal their secret identities. In the end, do they reconcile their double lives or do they decide to keep their secret identity hidden? What life lessons might this momentous decision ultimately impart to tween viewers?

Themes found in live-action TV sitcoms targeting tweens may focus on unbelievable conceits, such as superheroes and villains living among us, or the neighbor next door secretly being a spy, but they provide a space to think about what it means to be a superhero or a villain and *why* people keep secrets. Perhaps the real secret these shows are portraying is not just so out-of-the ordinary. As *Hannah Montana* puts it, "I know changing can be scary, but it's a part of growing up. It's how we find out who we are and who we're gonna be."

2 Tweens, Teens, and TV

In a 2021 census of media use by tweens and teens, Common Sense Media found that 8- to 12-year olds use an average of 5 and a half hours of screen media per day, and 13- to 18-year olds use around 8 and a half hours of screen media (Common Sense Media 2022). Young people use screens to do their homework, connect with others through social media, play games, and watch videos on YouTube. While screens facilitate various endeavors for young people, a major portion of young people's screen time is spent watching "traditional" TV programming. Common Sense notes: "Watching television still occupies more time in young people's media diets than any other single media activity. … Tweens watch about an hour and a half of television daily (1:36), and teens average closer to two hours a day (1:50)" (Common Sense Media 2022). Young people may watch TV on an actual TV through traditional broadcast and cable channels or through various streaming channels; or they may watch on their phone, tablet, or computer. They have access to a library of a plethora of programs that spans much of TV's history. *Variety* notes that young people are no longer watching media in a traditional, linear way, which is evidenced by a decrease in network viewing numbers (Schneider, 2023). However, given the previously cited Common Sense Media statistics, it stands to reason that while tweens are not necessarily watching shows when they are first broadcast in prime-time, they are still consuming the content, just in a non-linear, more "on-demand" manner.

Given the ubiquity of TV today, it is astounding to think that it was less than a hundred years ago that TV was introduced to American families. When the first TV sets were commercially produced for the public in 1938, the concept of "tweens" did not even exist. TV programming did not really become popular until after World War II, once the economy was in recovery and families could both afford a TV set and begin to enjoy more leisure time. It is important to remember that TV at this time was broadcast live. This is critical for a few reasons: 1) because it was broadcast, you needed to be geographically near to a facility that was broadcasting the signal. This meant that major cities had the majority of viewers; 2)

DOI: 10.4324/9781003593027-2

programming was meant for a broad array of viewers, hence the term broadcasting; and 3) there were no recordings at this time: if you didn't see it when it was broadcast live, you never saw it.

According to *The American Century*, in 1950 just 9% of households owned a TV set, and by 1954 55.7% did. That is a 519% increase in just 4 years. In 1963 over 90% of households owned TVs, and by 1978 98% of homes had TV sets (The American Century n.d.).

Even though early American TV programs were created for a general audience, some were likely more popular with young people than others. These shows varied in genre, from game shows such as *Truth or Consequences* (1950), to dramas like *Lassie* (1954), variety programs including *The Mickey Mouse Club* (1955), and sitcoms such as *Leave It to Beaver* (1957). Given the popularity of TV with children, it isn't surprising that shows targeted specifically to children began to grow in popularity. *Captain Kangaroo* (1955) and *Romper Room* (1953) were aimed at preschool children, while *Bozo the Clown* (1949) and *Howdy Doody* (1947) were targeted to school-aged kids.

Bozo the Clown and *Romper Room* were also popular because they capitalized on the concept of franchising local productions. Rather than being dependent on having one national program being broadcast through local stations via syndication, *Bozo the Clown* and *Romper Room* franchised their concept – and likeness in the case of Bozo – to be produced on local stations. This allowed for a much broader reach.

Together with *Howdy Doody*, *Bozo the Clown* also introduced a key ingredient that highlighted a major opportunity available in the marketing shows specifically to young people – merchandising.

Besides merchandising, other production practices were evolving that contributed to the growth of TV productions specifically targeting children. The 1957 invention of video tape allowed programs to air "live to tape" which also allowed for the preservation of broadcasts for posterity. There were still no reruns or the DVR, or even the VCR yet, but this did allow for more quantity of productions as well as the possibility of rebroadcasting past programs.

As stated earlier, by 1963 over 90% of American homes had a TV. Programming practices had Saturday mornings carved out for children's programs and weeknights were considered "family viewing." Even though 90% of homes had a TV, it was just ONE TV for the entire family – rather than one per room in the house like today. So, in the 1960s, during the week, families were watching shows like *Beverly Hillbillies* or *The Andy Griffith Show*. These family-focused sitcoms featured idealized or fantasy versions of family that were viewed by the entire family. This was really the beginning of "appointment TV".

For ABC, this family viewing was used as a programming strategy where they programmed family-friendly shows on Friday nights. Examples included *The Adventures of Ozzie and Harriet*, *Leave It to Beaver*, and *The Donna Reed Show* in the late 1950s. This strategy continued into the 1970s with the Friday-night scheduling of *The Brady Bunch* and *The Partridge Family*. All of these sitcoms were not only family-friendly but also focused on different takes on the family dynamic. In the late 1980s the evolution of ABC's family-friendly Friday nights led to a branding campaign of "TGIF" which played on the phrase "Thank God it's Friday" and redubbed it "Thank Goodness its Funny." The F in TGIF could very well have also stood for "family" as the sitcoms in this programming block featured different configurations of families and were marketed to be watched as a family for the entire block of programming (typically four shows).

The original programs in the TGIF block were *Perfect Strangers*, *Full House*, *Mr. Belvedere* and *Just the Ten of Us*. Over the years other shows that were part of ABC's TGIF programming block included *Family Matters*, *Step by Step*, *Boy Meets World*, and *Sabrina the Teenage Witch*, among others.

This block programming strategy was likely a response to the growth of cable and its programming strategies. The concept of delivering programming through cable rather than broadcast signal had been around since the early days of American TV, when it was difficult to receive a broadcast signal. However, the growth of cable as not just distribution channel, but also a source of programming for entertainment programming did not happen until the late 1970s, with Home Box Office (HBO), and didn't become popular until the late 1980s. When TGIF launched in the fall of 1988, a little over half of U.S. households had cable (CCTA, n.d.).

The growth of cable led to a specialization of content – or narrowcasting of content. Rather than trying to reach everyone, as broadcast channels did, cable companies could target specific, niche markets, like news (such as CNN), sports (like ESPN), music (for example, MTV), and children's TV. The first two children's cable TV channels were Nickelodeon and Disney Channel.

The Nickelodeon cable channel launched on April 1, 1979, and is considered the first cable channel for children. Over the years, Nickelodeon has further segmented its target audience through the creation of NickToons, Nick Jr., and TeenNick. Paramount reports that Nickelodeon reaches more than 20 million households, and has been the number one rated basic cable network for 20 consecutive years (Paramount n.d.). Currently, the Nickelodeon library of shows can be streamed on Paramount+. As of June, 2022, Paramount+ had 43.3 million subscribers (Variety 2022b).

Three years after the introduction of Nickelodeon, The Walt Disney Company unveiled its rival children's cable channel: Disney Channel. Since 1997, it has been known simply as Disney Channel. Like Nickelodeon, it has subdivided into Disney Junior, Toon Disney, and Disney XD. In 2014,

Disney Channel had almost 2 million average viewers, but that number has declined, as more people use Disney+. The Disney Channel library of programs is available on Disney+. In October, 2022, there were 164.2 million subscribers to Disney+ (Variety 2022a).

The subdivision of these children's cable channels illustrates partitioning of childhood in general. No longer were we talking about "children" in a broad sense, but rather now we were segmenting childhood into preschool, school-aged, pre-teen, and teenagers. And as childhood was subdivided, increasing attention was given to the market of school-aged and pre-teen children, who were dubbed "tweens." In a 2004 *Newsweek* article titled, "Tweens: Marketing's Gold Mine," Romano described the battle between Nickelodeon and Disney Channel and alluded to the importance of the "lucrative 9-14 demographic" and quoted executives using the term tween. This was one of the earliest mentions of "tween" in children's TV. But where did this term come from?

If you search back into the etymology of the word, tween was used as far back as c. 1300 as an abbreviation of between, and was even used by Tolkien in *The Lord of the Rings* to describe the "irresponsible twenties between [Hobbits'] childhood and coming of age at thirty-three. But the modern use of the term tween to refer to children who aren't quite teens yet but aren't "little kids" either didn't start until the late 1980s (Etymonline n.d.). According to Emily Aguilio-Perez (2017), the term tween was first used in a 1987 article in *Marketing and Media Decisions*. In that article, it was used to describe a market of children between the ages of 9 and 15. While the term was used in 1987, the practice of marketing to this group became popularized in the early 2000s. In the abstract for his 2003 research article, "Branding is no longer child's play" in *The Journal of Consumer Marketing*, Martin Lindstrom writes: "Tweens (8–14-year-olds) comprise a new type of audience – an increasingly powerful and smart consumer group which last year alone spent and influenced an astounding US$ 1.18 trillion across the globe. They are different in every way … building brands to our future generation no longer is just a child's play" (2003, 175).

While marketers and TV executives recognize the opportunities of promoting to a tween audience, it is also important to understand tweens as more than simply a market or audience. Who are tweens? WHY are they such a unique audience?

For a long time in children's TV, programming focused mainly on pedagogical learning. The best example of this is the quintessential children's TV show, *Sesame Street*. When *Sesame Street* became popular in the 1970s, the content of the show was designed to teach children their ABCs and 123s in a fun and exciting manner. This was modeled by broadcast channels in Saturday morning programming such as *Schoolhouse Rock*. As early as 1971, we saw an attempt to reach older children and their learning with *The Electric Company*. Later, *Zoom* would target even older kids. The challenge in reaching this demographic is balancing business, entertainment, and education. With tweens, there is less focus on pedagogical learning and more on learning about life and finding their place in the world. This mirrors what is happening to youth during these times of development. Child development theorists Erikson and Piaget agree on the importance of social interactions (which would include mediated interactions) to the development of self.

In Erikson's Eight Stages of Psychosocial Development (1950), he describes the period of 6–12 years as the "Industry versus Inferiority" stage. He posits that the school years are a time of comparison. It stands that this comparison would not only be with their peers, but also with characters they watch regularly on TV. The effect this comparison has on children's self-esteem is of particular importance. According to Erikson, adolescence is all about developing a sense of self. In adolescence this is also marked by the tension between autonomy of the individual and attachment to their parents. Young people are searching to find their own identity and make their own decisions while simultaneously nurturing relationships with their family and peers (Erikson 1950).

Piaget's Stages of Cognitive Development Theory (1972) explains how children actively adjust their own understandings as they learn about the world through assimilation and accommodation of schemas. Schemas are everything someone already knows about a particular subject or idea. Assimilation is the process of bringing new information into a schema that already exists in the mind. Accommodation is the process of adjusting or adapting a scheme, so it better fits the experience. Accommodation and assimilation are markedly different during different stages of development. Tweens would fall into Piaget's third stage, Concrete Operational Thought (Ages 7–11), and the beginning of the fourth stage, Formal Operational Thought (Age 12 and Above). According to Piaget (1972), Concrete Operational Thought is a stage of cognitive development where children solidify their abstract thinking and begin to understand cause and effect and logical implications of actions. By the Formal Operational Thought stage, they begin to plan for the future, think hypothetically, and assume adult responsibilities.

So, given this stage of life, when tweens are actively comparing themselves to their peers and developing their own sense of autonomy, it isn't surprising that there have been – and continue to be – a number of programs that allow tweens to explore what Markus and Nurius (1986) call "possible selves." They describe this type of self-knowledge as how individuals think about their potential and about their future. "Possible selves are the ideal selves that we would very much like to become. They are also the selves we could become and the selves we are afraid of becoming" (Markus and Nurius 1986, 954). Perhaps they can see these possible selves in the TV programming they view. In 2004 a former Disney entertainment president, Rich Ross, explained that Disney produces shows *for* tween-aged kids, but the shows feature older teen-aged kids in order to create aspirations for the viewers (Romano 2004, 17). These aspirations contribute to tween's possible selves.

Both developmental stage theories and the theory of possible selves focus on tweens' self-knowledge and self-identity – finding out who they are, what they value, and what they want for their future. While we are all continuously on a journey of self-knowledge and self-identity, the period of early adolescence launches us on our quest for self-discovery.

Given how consequential "tweenhood" is in our development, it is not surprising to see that once the market segmentation of children's cable channels occurred, shows that targeted tweens featured characters and stories that create a sandbox for tweens to play around in and explore possible selves. Possible selves are especially applicable to a particular subgenre of tween TV – live-action sitcoms that feature characters with a secret identity or leading a double life. Wrapped in these stories of secret identities and double lives are models of what tweenhood is like: finding your own voice, the tension between autonomy and attachment to your family, and negotiating interpersonal relationships with family and friends. So why are secret identities and double lives such a popular vehicle for this? To answer this, we need to first take a closer look at the trope of secret identities and double lives in general.

References

The American Century. n.d. "Number of TV Households in American 1950–1978." https://americancentury.omeka.wlu.edu/items/show/136.

Aguilio-Perez, Emily, 2017. "Tweens." Oxford Bibliographies in Childhood Studies. https://www.oxfordbibliographies.com/display/document/obo-9780199791231/obo-9780199791231-0189.xml

CCTA(California Cable & Telecommunications Association). n.d. History of Cable. https://calcable.org/learn/history-of-cable/.

Common Sense Media. 2022. "The Common Sense Census: Media Use by Tweens and Teens, 2021." https://www.commonsensemedia.org/research/the-common-sense-census-media-use-by-tweens-and-teens-2021.

Erikson, Erik. 1950. *Childhood and Society*. W.W. Norton & Co.

Lindstrom, Martin. 2003. "Branding is No Longer Child's Play." *Journal of Consumer Marketing*, *21* (3), 175–182.

Markus, Hazel and Nurius, Paula. 1986. "Possible Selves." *American Psychologist*, *41* (9) 954–969.

Online Etymology Dictionary, n.d. "tween". https://www.etymonline.com/word/tween.

Paramount. n.d. "The #1 Entertainment Brand for Kids." https://www.paramount.com/brand/nickelodeon.

Piaget, Jean, and Barbel Inhelder. 1972. *The Psychology of the Child*. New York, NY: Basic Books.

Romano, A. (2004, August 16). Tweens: Marketing's gold mine. *Newsweek*, 144(7), 38–44.

Schneider, Michael. (2023). Most-watched television networks: Ranking 2023's winners and losers. *Variety*. December 28, 2023.

Variety. 2022a. "Disney+ Adds 12.1 Million Subscribes to Cross 164 Million Worldwide Ahead of Ad-Tier Launch." https://variety.com/2022/tv/news/disney-plus-subscribers-164-million-1235426552/

Variety. 2022b. "Paramount+ Tops 43 Million Subscribers in Q2, Adding 3.7 Million in Quarter." https://variety.com/2022/digital/news/paramount-plus-q2-2022-subscribers-1235332550/

3 Secret Identities

To better understand the popularity of secret identity stories in live-action tween TV sitcoms, it is essential to first understand the trope of secret identities in general. Before we delve deeper into the trope of secret identities, though, let's back up and make sure we understand what a trope is and why they are popular on TV.

A trope is a storytelling device. It's a shortcut that a storyteller uses because they assume that their audience will recognize the situation to which the trope refers. According to Dictionary.com, the word trope was first recorded in 1525–35 – from Latin *tropus* meaning "figure in rhetoric, manner of singing" and from Greek *trópos* meaning "turn, manner, style, figure of speech." Tropes can be used for most parts of storytelling including character, setting, plot, and theme.

Some popular theme tropes in literature and film include atonement or redemption, the love triangle, best friends–turned lovers, and rags to riches, to name just a few. Because of the serialized nature of TV sitcoms, they are even more reliant on tropes. Sitcoms are dependent on easily understandable storylines and situations. These live-action tween sitcoms are a mix and match of many tropes.

Telling an engaging story in 22 minutes on a weekly basis can be challenging. There is not always time to develop backstory and nuance, so tropes are an efficient storytelling device. Besides the secret identity trope, other tropes that resound with tweens include school tropes, friend tropes, sibling tropes, and parent tropes (tvtropes.org n.d.-a).

Tvtropes.org is a wiki that catalogs TV tropes by category, identifies tropes in story, character, and situation. They highlight school tropes that involve types of schools (for example, "cool school," "ghoul school," "spy academy," or "hero academy"); students in the school (such as "child prodigy," "big jerk on campus," "class clown," and "cool loser"); relationships between students (for instance "high school sweethearts," "girl posse," or "eating lunch alone"); and school events (like "class reunion," "homecoming," "the prom," or "Science Fair"), to just scratch the surface (tvtropes.org n.d.-b).

DOI: 10.4324/9781003593027-3

The tropes tracked by tvtropes.org relating to friends are vast and range from "Imaginary Friend" to "Fire-Forged Friends" and relate to specific episodes, types of friendships, and friendship situations. Sibling tropes also abound, and feature types of siblings (sister/brother, older/younger, step, half, foster, and more), as well as sibling situations, such as "Black Sheep," "Promotion to Parent," and "parental favoritism" (tvtropes.org n.d.-c).

Parents are also featured in their own set of tropes, that range from parenting style, like "Hands-off Parenting" or "Pushover Parents," to types of parents, like "Stage Mom," "Struggling Single Mother," or "Sports Dad," as well as situational, such as "Strict Parents Make Sneaky Kids," "Parents are Wrong," or "Not Under the Parents' Roof" (tvtropes.org n.d.-d).

These friends and family tropes will interact with the Secret Identity and Double-Lives trope in later chapters. But first, it is critical to understand just what the secret identity and double-lives trope are and why it is so popular in tween TV.

It is widely accepted that one of the earliest literary uses of the secret identity trope was in *The Scarlet Pimpernel* in 1903. In Baroness Orczy's play (and then book) the Scarlett Pimpernel was the secret identity of Sir Percy Blakeney. In his secret life, Sir Blakeney rescues aristocrats from the guillotine using his skills with the sword and a bevy of disguises and is known only by the flower he uses to identify himself, the scarlet pimpernel. The contrast of his two identities – the daring pimpernel with the unassuming Blakeney – was very popular at that time, and this contrast has been emulated by many in the future, with characters such as Zorro, Superman, and Batman, to name just a few.

Superheroes have been the most prolific beneficiaries of the secret identity trope. Just as with the Scarlet Pimpernel, the public knows of the deeds of Superman, Batman, Spiderman, Wonder Woman, and so on, but they are not necessarily familiar with Clark Kent, Bruce Wayne, Peter Parker, or Diana Prince. Given that, it is really their private life that is the secret identity. This separation of public and private identities provides the alternate moniker for this trope – double lives. The two terms, secret identity and double lives, are essentially the same thing and will be used interchangeably in this book. This should not be confused with an alter ego – or a form of self that one is not aware of, such as Dr. Jekyll and Mr. Hyde. In the double-lives trope, the characters are knowingly separating their two identities for a variety of reasons. They are usually protecting someone – themselves, their friends, or their family – from the actions of their "other self," or in the case of superheroes or vigilantes, they are protecting themselves from legal ramifications.

While superheroes may be the most well-known use of the secret/double identity trope in today's culture, it is by no means the only one. This is made evident when looking at the subject of this book – double lives in live-action tween TV. On these programs there are some superheroes, but there are also bionic teens, supervillains, spies, wizards, witches, and a pop star. Later in this chapter, a brief description of each of these programs and the double life/secret identity it features will be provided. But it is first important to discuss why there might be so many secret identity-focused programming on live-action tween TV.

If you take the concept of double lives and secret identities and cross it with the identity exploration period of adolescence, it is not surprising that over the years there have been a number of programs with this premise. The concept of "possible selves" was introduced in the last chapter. To briefly review, according to Markus and Nurius (1986), possible selves allow us to explore who we are, who we want to be, and who we fear to be. Possible selves are just one aspect of the self-identity journey young people embark on during adolescence. One of the most important characteristics of a young person's identity exploration is the dialectic of autonomy and attachment: the tension between becoming their own person and their connection to family and peers. The popularity of programs that feature adolescents who are navigating a secret identity could be attractive to tweens because while they might not be balancing double lives, they are still straddling the line between the child they have been so far and the teenager they are about to become. While tweens struggle to find themselves, it can be reassuring to escape into worlds where characters are truly hiding who they are and explore what occurs. The live-action sitcoms analyzed for this book target a tween audience and feature characters who are actively balancing double lives. The original broadcast dates of these programs range from 1996 to the present; however, all of these shows are currently available for viewers to watch through streaming services. The following paragraphs will briefly describe each of the 11 shows that were investigated, with specific focus on the secret identity featured. They will be discussed in chronological order, from the show that aired the earliest to the most current. (A full description of each show, including cast and episode names, can be found in the Appendix.)

Sabrina the Teenage Witch debuted on ABC on September 27, 1996, as part of the TGIF lineup. It ran for seven seasons total, four on ABC and three on the WB. During its run on ABC, it averaged 12–17 million viewers per episode. The program was based on the character from the Archie comic series. On her 16th birthday, Sabrina Spellman learns that she is a witch and has magical powers. Sabrina lives with her aunts, Hilda and Zelda, and attends high school. Sabrina has to learn to navigate her new magical powers and keep them secret from the outside world. While on ABC, Sabrina tackled typical teen angst comparable to the other shows in the sample. When it moved to the WB, Sabrina went to college and then got a job, and therefore deviated from the sample a bit.

Like Sabrina, Miley Stewart has a secret. In her other life, she is Hannah Montana, international pop star. *Hannah Montana*, debuted on March 24, 2006, on Disney Channel and ran for four seasons, averaging 5 million viewers per episode (Associated Press, 2010). Miley wants to live a normal life, so she created her Hannah Montana persona for her music career. When the show begins, Miley is starting her freshman year in high school. She lives with her father and brother in Malibu, California. Her mother has passed away. She has two best friends, Lily and Oliver. To complicate things, both Lily and Oliver are huge Hannah Montana fans.

A little over year after *Hannah Montana* premiered, Disney Channel launched *The Wizards of Waverly Place* on October 12, 2007, which ran for four seasons and averaged approximately 4 million viewers an episode (Walsh Boyle, 2010). On this program, the Russo siblings, Justin, Alex and Max, are all learning magic and competing to become the one family wizard. Wizard law and custom allow only one member of every family to be a wizard. Their father, Jerry Russo, was a wizard when he was younger. However, he gave up his powers to his brother so that he could marry Justin, Alex, and Max's mom, Therese. Still, he is in charge of the wizarding education of his children up until the family wizard competition. The family must keep the children's wizardry a secret, to protect the wizarding world.

Five years after *The Wizards of Waverly Place* premiered, on February 27, 2012, Disney XD debuted another show featuring characters with secret identities, *Lab Rats* – which also ran for four seasons. In *Lab Rats*, teenager Leo Dooley discovers that his new billionaire genius stepfather, Donald Davenport, has three bionic, super-human teens – Adam, Bree, and Chase – living in his basement. Leo and his new "step-siblings" eventually all attend Mission Creek Jr./Sr. High School and have to "pass" as being normal kids. Adam, Bree, and Chase balance life at school with going on missions led by Davenport. Disney XD was a more niche channel, and the show never broke more than 1 million viewers.

A year and a half later and also on Disney XD, *Mighty Med* premiered on October 7, 2013, and ran for two seasons. Middle-school best friends Kaz and Oliver discover a secret hospital for superheroes and start to work there. They must keep this a secret to protect all of the superheroes. They develop a close relationship with Skylar Storm, a superhero patient at Mighty Med who has had her powers taken away by a villain. Eventually Skylar attends Logan High School with Kaz and Oliver and has to keep her superhero identity a secret. The main characters also develop a close relationship with Dr. Horace Diaz, who is Mighty Med's chief of staff. He acts as a type of mentor to the "normos" Kaz and Oliver. This leads to an antagonistic relationship with Dr. Diaz's nephew, Alan, who becomes jealous. In 2016, the *Mighty Med* characters Kaz, Oliver, and Skylar joined forces with Chase and Bree from *Lab Rats* in a new show, *Lab Rats*

Elite Force, which lasted just one season. As both programs were aired on Disney XD, they too had smaller niche viewership.

A week after *Mighty Med* premiered on Disney XD, on October 13, 2013, Nickelodeon launched their new superhero show, *The Thundermans*. *The Thundermans* featured a family of superheroes living in the town of Hiddenville. The two main protagonists are twins Max and Phoebe Thunderman who share powers of telekinesis, heat breath, and freeze breath. Max and Phoebe live in Hiddenville with their parents, Hank (Thunderman) and Barb (Electress), and their younger siblings Billy and Nora. In the second season finale, Barb has a baby, Chloe, who ages quickly since she is a superhero. For the first three seasons, Max was training to become a supervillain to differentiate himself from his twin, Phoebe, but he eventually decided to use his powers for good. Both Max and Phoebe attend Hiddenville High. The entire family moved to Hiddenville so that the children could have a "normal" life growing up. However, they struggle to suppress their superpowers, and still need to keep them secret from the rest of Hiddenville. *The Thundermans* ran on Nickelodeon for four seasons, with average viewership ranging from over 2 million during its first season to 1.47 million during the last season (The Futon Critic, 2014).

Nickelodeon continued to capitalize on the superhero trend by introducing another superhero-focused show, *Henry Danger*, on July 26, 2014. While *The Thundermans* focused on an entire family of superheroes, *Henry Danger* spotlighted one young boy, Henry Hart, who becomes the superhero sidekick, "Kid Danger," to superhero, Captain Man, after getting an after-school job with Captain Man's alter ego, Ray Manchester. Henry helps Captain Man fight crime while hiding his secret identity from his friends and family. Henry lives at home with his parents, Kris and Jake, and his younger sister, Piper. Henry has two best friends, Charlotte and Jasper. *Henry Danger* ran on Nickelodeon for five seasons and averaged 1.5 million viewers.

Another family who are all keeping secrets are the Coopers on *K.C. Undercover*, which premiered on Disney Channel on January 18, 2015, and ran for three seasons, with viewership ranging from 1.1 to 2.3 million viewers. K.C. is recruited by her parents to become a spy for a secret agency called The Organization. Eventually, K.C.'s brother, Ernie, joins the family business as well. K.C. and Ernie's parents bring home a robot – J.U.D.Y. (Junior Undercover Digital Youth) – that looks like an 8-year-old girl. Judy becomes part of the family – and a part of the family spy business as well. When not fighting crime with her family, K.C. is a gifted high-school student, and enjoys spending time with her best friend, Marisa Miller.

In 2022 there were two shows that premiered that feature characters leading double lives. Both *The Villains of Valley View* and *Ultra-Violet &*

Black Scorpion are Disney Channel shows that premiered together on June 3, 2022. *The Villains of Valley View* features a family of supervillains, The Maddens, who are hiding from The League of Villains and have to pass as a "normal" family. The Maddens live next door to their landlord, Celia and her granddaughter, Hartley. Hartley discovers the Maddens' secret and helps them assimilate into a "regular" life. *Ultra-Violet & Black Scorpion* centers around Violet Rodriguez, a 13-year old who gets chosen by a magical Luchador mask that transforms her into "Ultra-Violet." She discovers her uncle is the "Black Scorpion" and together they fight crime while hiding their secret identities. Violet lives with her parents, Nina and Juan Carlos, and her brother Santiago. Nina is the principal at Violet's school.

There is an interesting mix of types of secret identities in these programs: a pop star, a witch, wizard siblings, a spy family, villains, and super-heroes, and the justifications for why these identities are being kept secret are varied as well. This also relates to how the secret identities transpired – some characters were born with their secret identities, others chose theirs, and still others had their identities thrust upon them. Characters in *Wizards of Waverly Place*, *The Thundermans*, *Lab Rats*, and *The Villains of Valley View* have always known about their secret identities. The secret has been part of their overall identities their entire lives. While *Sabrina the Teenage Witch* had always been a witch, she didn't discover that news until her 16th birthday. That is very different from the protagonists of *Henry Danger*, *K.C. Undercover*, and *Mighty Med* who were given a choice to take the responsibility of their secret identities. Ultra-Violet was not given a choice regarding her powers or secret identity; rather she was chosen. The magical luchador mask selects Violet. Finally, Miley Stewart proactively creates the persona of Hannah Montana so that she can try to lead a normal life.

Another area where we can see differences related to secret identities is what people in these characters' lives know about their secret identities at the beginning of each series. In later chapters we will look at how this relates to relationships of family, friendship, and romance, as well as how the revelation of their secret identities to others affects themselves and others; but, for now, it is relevant to grasp a comparative understanding of how secret these secret identities really are when the programs commence.

In *Hannah Montana*, Miley's father and brother both know that Miley is also Hannah Montana, but none of her friends know. Similarly, in *Sabrina the Teenage Witch*, Sabrina's aunts and father know she is a witch – in fact, they are the ones who break that news to Sabrina herself. In *Wizards of Waverly Place*, the Russo siblings' parents know that they are wizards. Their father was once a wizard as well: he won the family wizarding competition when he was a teen, but he gave up his powers to his brother so he could marry his wife, who is mortal. All of the Thundermans know their secret, as do the Hero League, who monitors all the superheroes in the universe. The beginning premise of *Lab Rats* is "normal" kid, Leo, discovering his bionic step-siblings; so besides Leo and his mom, no one else knows about them. In *Mighty Med*, Kaz and Oliver are the only everyday citizens to know the secret of *Mighty Med*. The superheroes know that Kaz and Oliver are from the "regular" world. At the beginning of *Henry Danger*, no one but Captain Man knows Henry's secret. In *K.C. Undercover*, only K.C.'s parents are first aware of her secret identity, since they recruit her to work with them for The Organization. At the start of *The Villains of Valley View*, no one is aware that the Maddens are really a family of supervillains. Since Ultra-Violet becomes a superhero in the initial episode, there could not be other characters who could know about her.

Whether they've known about their "secret identity" all along, or if they've just discovered it; or if one, two, or more people know about it, what ties all of these programs together is the desire for the protagonists to keep their identities secret and to be seen by others as "normal." As discussed in the previous chapter, developmental psychologists concur that adolescence is a time of social comparison, so it is not surprising that this dominant theme of "fitting in" plays out in these programs.

As typical tweens and teens, these characters want to fit in with their peers, still they are also trying to differentiate themselves from their family units. This focus on autonomy is a perfect vehicle for the secret identity trope. Having the ability to control the two sides of themselves – more specifically who knows their "secret" side – gives these young characters a tremendous amount of power. Interestingly, power is one area that young people in "real" life feel much less than those in "reel" life. The next chapter will explore this further.

References

Associated Press (2010). Disney to cancel 'Hannah Montana' after season 4. *CTVNews*, January 8, 2010.

The Futon Critic. (2014). Saturday's cable ratings & broadcast finals. *The Futon Critic*. June 17, 2014.

Markus, Hazel and Nurius, Paula. 1986. "Possible Selves." *American Psychologist*, *41* (9) 954–969.

Orczy, Emuska. 1903. *The Scarlet Pimpernel*. Waiheke Island, Floating Press.

Tvtropes. n.d.-a Friendship Tropes. https://tvtropes.org/pmwiki.pmwiki.php/Main/FriendshipTropes

Tvtropes. n.d.-b The Parent Trope. https://tvtropes.org/pmwiki.pmwiki.php/Main/TheParentTrope

Tvtropes. n.d.-c Secret Identity. https://tvtropes.org/pmwiki.pmwiki.php/Main/SecretIdentity.

Tvtropes. n.d.-d High School. https://tvtropes.org/pmwiki.pmwiki.php/Main/HighSchool

Walsh Boyle, Megan. (2010). Exclusive: Disney Channel Announces Season 4 of Wizards of Waverly Place. *TV Guide*. October 14, 2010.

4 Power

Power is complex and hard to define. Still, when you have power, you are aware of it, and conversely, when you lack power, you are also cognizant of that. While most would agree that they know what power feels like, it is still difficult to describe in full. For one thing, there are different spheres of power such as cultural power, political power, interpersonal power, and personal power. The common denominator for all scopes of power is the ability to influence and exercise some type of control. For most young people, power is relevant because they are learning how to find their own personal power while still navigating a world where power is wielded by so many others: parents, teachers, and society in general.

This chapter does not set out to provide an exhaustive or even comprehensive look at power. Rather, those aspects of power relevant to tweens and teens and their journey of self-identity will be addressed and then connected to secret-lives tween shows.

Adolescence is marked by the passage from dependence into independence. While young people search to find out who they are, they are still tethered to their families. Therefore, a central aspect of power in the lives of tweens and teens centers on interpersonal power, or power in close relationships. Structuration Theory (Giddens 1984) identifies five different types of interpersonal power: reward power, coercive power, expert power, legitimate power, and referent power. Structuration Theory suggests that coercive power is based on the expectation that an individual has the ability to exact punishment. For tweens, this type of power is likely wielded by parents (i.e., "if you don't eat all your dinner, you don't get dessert), as well as teachers (i.e., "if you are late for class, you will get a demerit"). Both parents and teachers can also exert reward power. Reward power involves the perception that another person can provide some sort of positive reinforcement. This positive reinforcement could be something material (like an allowance from parents or grades from a teacher), or it could be something intangible, such as praise and positive body language. Both parents and teachers also have legitimate power, just based on their

DOI: 10.4324/9781003593027-4

position. Parents usually have legitimate power with their children and teachers hold legitimate power with their students. Expert power is differentiated not by the position of the person, but rather by their level of expertise and skill in some specific area (such as a doctor or a mechanic). The final type of power is usually the most coveted, yet it is the hardest to achieve. Referent power is established because of established personal relationships. A good example of this would be a coach whose players respect and admire them. They work hard, not because they are worried the coach will punish them, or because they know the coach can reward them, but rather because they WANT to work hard FOR the coach.

It is interesting to see how these interpersonal power dynamics play out in any TV programs, including these live-action tween sitcoms. The parent-child power dynamic will be discussed further in Chapter 9, but it's important to mention here, because parental figures endure as the primary power figure in young people's lives, no matter which type of power they possess.

When young people perceive that they hold no power in their own lives, it can lead to alienation. Sociologists explain that alienation is multifaceted. The most essential ingredient of alienation is powerlessness, or the feeling that one's own destiny is not under their own control. Alienation also incorporates meaninglessness, normlessness, cultural estrangement, social isolation, and self-estrangement. If you look at powerlessness and alienation on a continuum, you could consider everyday teen angst on one end of the spectrum and true alienation on the other. Calabrese (2000) explored alienation in adolescence and noted

> adolescence is a high-risk period wherein the adolescent experiences in multiple environments exacerbate higher levels of alienation. These environments include disorganized or disruptive families, schools that encourage students to become passive participants in the learning process, and a high-pressure pace of life.

But a teen or tween doesn't need to experience full-blown alienation to feel powerless. It is part of the process of adolescence to balance powerlessness and power. A good working definition of "typical" powerlessness comes from Wallston et al. as "the belief that one can[not] determine or control one's own internal states and behavior, influence one's environment, and/or bring about desired outcomes" (Wallston et al., 1987).

This feeling of lack of control and influence is emblematic of adolescence. Just when young people begin to learn to become self-sufficient and develop their own values and ideas, they are simultaneously being asked to follow the rules of their parents, their teachers, and others who hold legitimate power. This is complicated by the fact that they are forming integral friendships with peers and still negotiating relationships with their families. They are trying to figure out who they are, and there are so many variables involved in this quest.

In his poem, Oenone (1892), Alfred Lord Tennyson wrote, "Self-reverence, self-knowledge and self-control, these three alone lead life to sovereign power." Tennyson's "trinity of excellences" provide a valuable lesson in power – self-love, self-knowledge, and self-control. The trinity is deceptively simple and proves elusive to many young people. How do you make it through the journey of adolescence knowing who you are, loving that person, and exercising self-control? A number of the concepts that will be discussed in later chapters certainly contribute to one's ability to achieve this trinity – our sense of morality (Chapter 5), our relationships with friends (Chapter 6), and connections with our family (Chapters 8–10). That intangible FEELING of autonomy and control of one's own destiny play a role in self-identity and self-love. Yet it is one of the most mysterious aspects of self and adolescence. When does the switch "turn" from being dependent on others to wanting to control your life? It is not that simple. In fact, research has shown that attachment actually aids in autonomy. Deci and Ryan (1985) reviewed studies of autonomy and attachment and found a positive relationship between perceptions of autonomy and perceived quality of relatedness. The reviewed studies showed that supportive relationships enable relatedness. Balts and Silverberg (1994, p. 57) also found that

> the developmental task of adolescence seems to be a complicated one that calls for a negotiated balance between and emerging sense of self as a competent individual on the one hand, and transformed, but continued, feeling of connection with significant others on the other.

It is not a battle between autonomy and connectedness, but rather a balanced integration of the two. Striking that balance can aid tweens in finding their own sense of personal power.

Firestone (2009) suggests that

> Personal power is based on strength, confidence, and competence that individuals gradually acquire in the course of their development. It is self-assertion, and a natural, healthy striving for love, satisfaction, and meaning in one's interpersonal world. This type of power represents a movement toward self-realization and transcendent goals in life; its primary aim is mastery of self, not others. Personal power is more of an attitude or state of mind than an attempt to maneuver or control others. It is based on competence, vision, positive personal qualities, and service. When externalized it is likely to be more generous, creative and humane than other forms of power.
>
> (Firestone, 2009, p. 1)

So, in looking at power in tween secret identity programs, it is essential to look at both interpersonal power and personal power. How do characters exert power over others, and how do they find power within themselves? Conversely, when do these characters feel powerless? Are there other people in their lives that contribute to this feeling of powerlessness? What might these answers teach tween viewers on their own journey of personal power?

The most obvious exhibition of power is on those shows that feature characters with some type of extraordinary power. This would include the witches of *Sabrina the Teenage Witch*; the Russo siblings on *The Wizards of Waverly Place*; the superheroes on *Henry Danger*, *The Thundermans*, *Mighty Med*, and *Ultra-Violet & Black Scorpion*; the supervillains on *The Villains of Valley View*; and the bionic teens of *Lab Rats*.

Sabrina Spellman learns she is a witch on her 16th birthday. As a witch, she can levitate, move from one location to another, conjure people and things, change things (transmogrification) into something else, slow time, and cast various spells. Similarly, wizards Alex, Justin, and Max Russo can all levitate, transform, teleport, freeze time, and cast spells. In addition, they can shape-shift, clone, and use telekinesis (move things with their mind). It's not surprising that the ability to change things through magic would be popular in tween shows, given the previous discussion of lack of autonomy in tweens. What tween wouldn't want the ability to freeze time, transform things, and cast spells? Still, even these characters that possess magical powers feel powerless at times. Sometimes, these characters literally have their powers taken away from them by an entity of higher power. For Sabrina, it is the Witches Council, and for the Russos of *The Wizards of Waverly Place* it is the Wizards Council. These councils represent the sociological structures and institutions that hold power in all adolescents' lives, such as school and the government. Still, it is when their loved ones are most in danger, and magic cannot save them, that we see magical beings feeling most vulnerable. While this happens a number of times for Alex Russo, the most memorable is in the two-part series finale. In these episodes, Alex's parents, best friend, and boyfriend are all imprisoned by an evil wizard. Alex is desperate to save them, but her magic doesn't help the situation. In the end, she sacrifices her powers to rescue them. This will be a reoccurring theme in many of these shows – family and friends are more important than anything else.

Superheroes do not have magic, but they do have special powers. When Henry Hart chews a specific type of gumball, he transforms into Kid Danger. Kid Danger is an excellent fighter, who utilizes numerous gadgets to fight crime. He also possesses the ability to cast a protective force field.

The Thundermans all possess specific superpowers. Dad Hank, or Thunderman, can fly and possesses super-strength. Mom Barb, or Electress, can harness the power of electricity and lightning. Youngest sibling Chloe, or Thundergirl, can teleport. Nora, or Laser Girl, possesses laser vision, while their brother, Billy, or Kid Quick, has super-speed. Twins Phoebe and Max both possess ice and heat breath as well as telekinesis.

When Violet Santiago dons her luchador mask, she exhibits super-speed as Ultra-Violet. Similarly, her uncle has super-strength when he wears his mask as Black Scorpion.

The supervillains of *The Villains of Valley View* are similar in that they each possess specific superpowers. Father Vic Madden is Brainiac, who has super-intelligence. Mom Eva Madden is Surge, who also harnesses electricity (it must be a mom thing!). Son Jake/Chaos possesses super-strength and sister Amy/Havoc can manipulate sound and sound waves. Their brother Colby/Flashform discovers his superpower, shapeshifting, or kinetic manipulation, at the beginning of the series. Towards the end of the first season, it is discovered that Colby is "the chosen one," a once-in-a-generation supervillain who has more than one superpower. Colby exhibits super-speed, invisibility, and teleportation too.

While the bionic teens on *Lab Rats* are not technically superheroes, they were given specific bionic powers. They all have multiple bionic abilities. Adam can breathe underwater and has heat vision, super-strength, and durability. Bree has super-speed, durability, and invisibility and can manipulate her voice. Chase exhibits super-intelligence and super-senses and can generate a force field of protection.

Whether these characters harness magic or superpowers, for all of these characters, these extraordinary abilities are a major part of their identity. They don't just HAVE a superpower; they ARE superheroes or supervillains. They don't just USE magic spells; they ARE witches and wizards. This will be important to keep in mind as we consider the interconnectedness of their public personas and their secret identities. They are hiding a major part of what makes them, THEM. For tween viewers who are figuring out who they are and perhaps struggling to share parts of their core selves with others, watching how these characters maneuver through their universes and come to terms with their true selves can be educational.

Mighty Med is a little bit different, in that the main protagonists, Kaz and Oliver, are regular teens who work at a superhero hospital. There are numerous superheroes that come through the halls of Mighty Med, but Skylar Storm is the only regular superhero character. Skylar Storm had 24 different superpowers, but all of them were taken away by the supervillain, the Annihilator. Watching Skylar adapt to losing all of her superpowers and adapt to becoming a "normo" allows viewers an exaggerated and amplified look into powerlessness. Skylar reconciles that she is no longer who she once was and decides that she needs to acclimate to life in the "real world." She retains her core sense of self, and wants to help others, but finds other ways to make that happen.

While the majority of the programs feature characters who possess a superior power or ability, there are two shows in which the characters do not: *K.C. Undercover* and *Hannah Montana*. *K.C. Undercover*, on the one hand, closely resembles a superhero show, because as spies K.C. and her family use gadgets to fight "the bad guys." Still, they do not have superpowers or wield magic. They are extremely smart, strong, and brave, but they are just "regular" people. They've created their power through their own hard work. They keep their identity as spies secret, because that is what spies do.

Hannah Montana, on the other hand, does not exhibit the same traditional power as these other programs. Miley Stewart's alter ego, Hannah Montana, enjoys a different type of power – cultural, celebrity power. Hannah sells out concerts, has paparazzi following her, is on the cover of magazines, and even meets the Queen of England. At her young age she has people working for her and people fighting to meet her. But at school, Miley is just like everyone else. She doesn't receive any special treatment. In this way, she is similar to the superheroes, supervillains, spies, witches, and wizards. ALL of these characters have to hide their powers.

This hiding is relevant to tweens because since they are just beginning to discover who they are, they are watching what happens when you hide your true self. That true self could be your sexuality, your intelligence, your family life, or your likes and dislikes. In today's society, that authentic self is even further complicated by social media. Perhaps a tween is living one life online and hiding something in their offline life. ANYTHING. We will revisit this in the final chapter of the book when we discuss if, when, and how these characters reveal their true identities.

Besides the overt portrayals of power found in these programs, power is also exerted through the choices the major characters make. It is important to remember that while these characters are pop stars, spies, supervillains, superheroes, wizards, and witches, they are still teens. A major part of being a teen is figuring out your value system and developing your moral compass. This will be explored further in the next chapter.

References

Balts, Margret M. and Silverberg, Susan B. (1994). The dynamics between dependency and autonomy: Illustrations across the life span. *Life-Span Development and Behavior*, Routledge.

Calabrese, Raymond L. 2000. "Alienation" in *Encyclopedia of Psychology*, *1* (1) 116–118.

Deci, Edward and Richard Ryan 1985. *Intrinsic Motivation and Self-Determination in Human Behavior*. New York: Plenum.

Firestone, Robert W. 2009. "Person Power" in Psychology Today. https://www.psychologytoday.com/us/blog/the-human-experience/200904/personal-power

Giddens, Anthony. 1984. *The Constitution of Society. Outline of the Theory of Structuration*. University of California Press, Berkeley.

Tennyson, Alfred T. (1892). *The death of Oenone, and other poems*. New York: Macmillan. Retrieved from Library of Congress.

Wallston, Kenneth A., Wallston, Barbara S., Smith, Shelton, and Dobbins, Carolyn (1987). Perceived control and health. *Current Psychology, 6* 5–25.

5 Morality

Assor (2012) explains that "to feel autonomous, we need to see ourselves as having self-guiding ideas, knowledge, sentiments, and preferences." He describes that we have an authentic inner compass (AIC) that informs us on what is truly important to us, and what we really value and need. Assor suggests that our AIC schemas (cognitive framework) inform us on how to proactively choose actions, relationships, and environments that will make us feel valuable and most satisfied. Our AIC schemas also pilot our reactions when we are unexpectedly presented with difficult or unfamiliar conditions. But how do these AIC schemas form? Psychologists explain that schemas are cognitive frameworks or concepts that help organize and interpret information. We use schemas because they allow us to take shortcuts in interpreting the vast amount of information that is available in our environment.

We start to develop our moral schemas early in life. As we develop, we need to learn the difference between right and wrong and how to act on that knowledge – in other words, we need to learn morality. Morality encompasses reasoning, emotions, and behavior – what we THINK about what is right and wrong, as well as how we FEEL about it and ACT on it.

Kohlberg (1981) uses a level and stage model to explain how we develop our moral reasoning. He describes three levels: Pre-conventional, Conventional, and Post-conventional. Each of these levels consists of two stages. Pre-conventional encompasses Stages 1 and 2, Conventional has Stages 3 and 4, and Post-conventional has Stages 5 and 6. Kohlberg explains that in Stage 1 of the Pre-conventional level we learn through punishment and obedience orientation. Imagine a 2-year-old being scolded "No! Don't do that! Bad boy!!" The child listens to his parents because they have the power. This relates to last chapter's discussion of coercive and reward power. As we move into Stage 2 of the Pre-conventional level, we start to learn how following rules serves our own needs. This stage is characterized by individualism, instrumental purpose, and exchange. We not only see how rules help us, but we also become aware that others have needs and interests too, and they may not match

DOI: 10.4324/9781003593027-5

our own. This stage relies heavily on exchange. A young child might obey their parent when asked to share a toy with a sibling because their parent says "If you share we can go to the park!"

Once children start to move out of just thinking about what is "in it for them" they've moved into the Conventional Level of Moral Reasoning. Stage 3 involves "mutual interpersonal expectations, relationships, and interpersonal conformity" (Kohlberg, 1981). During this time in their lives, children are concerned about what others think. They want to live up to other's expectations of them. They are learning about being loyal and trustworthy and consider their intentions and those of others. So that same child will share with their sibling because they want their parent to know they are "good" and because they want to make that sibling feel happy. As they move into Stage 4, the second stage of the Conventional Level, their world broadens past their family into the larger social world. Our sharing child will not only share with their sibling, but with a classmate as well. They are learning what societal expectations are and how to fulfill them.

Once a person learns expectations of right and wrong they move into Kohlberg's third level, Post-conventional. During Stage 5, people begin to understand that values and rules are relative to particular groups and can be changed. They may begin to question the reasonings for obeying certain rules, and considering if the rules are just and fair. In Stage 6, the final stage of moral reasoning, a person develops and follows their own set of ethical principles and value system. If societal laws violate those principles, the person's actions will be consistent with their own values. Not everyone reaches this stage of moral reasoning.

Kohlberg's research found that Stage 3 of moral reasoning peaks during the mid-teens and Stage 4 increases considerably during adolescence. These are the stages that most of the viewers of these secret-identity tween sitcoms inhabit, and the stages that the teen characters are also living in. The moral reasoning of the characters and that of their audience are heavily influenced by others, primarily their families and peers, but to some extent society as whole. Arguably, the characters themselves can be influential to the tween audience's sense of morality.

One concept that becomes important in adolescence and relates to the Conventional stage of morality is perspective-taking. Perspective-taking is the ability to understand the psychological perspective, motives, and needs of others. It is central to the development of moral reasoning, and plays a major role in learning empathy, prosocial reasoning, altruism, and aggression as well. Learning to put yourself in another person's "shoes" is a critical aspect of moral development. As children grow into adolescence, they start to reason pro-socially; they think about helping others. The motivation behind why they help others is important to consider. Are they helping others in an expectation of some sort of external reward or punishment, or are they doing it out of true altruism? Conversely, if they behave aggressively toward others, what is the likely motivation? Deci and Ryan's (1985) Self-Determination Theory would argue that motivations are central to all behaviors – positive and negative. Self-Determination Theory explores both intrinsic and extrinsic motivations and is closely connected to a person's autonomy competence and relatedness to others. So, it really is all intertwined – a person's sense of self and relationship with others influence their moral reasoning, which in turn will contribute to their sense of self and will impact how they treat others as well.

Besides learning from others, another part of the process of learning about morality and finding your AIC involves making mistakes. What's interesting about secret identity tween shows is that moral struggle between right and wrong and the mistakes characters make because those struggles play out on a much larger scale in the "reel" world, in comparison to the "real" world.

When a witch or wizard breaks a rule, there can be serious consequences. When a superhero becomes tempted to use their powers for personal gain, there can be unforeseen ramifications. The remainder of this chapter will explore how these and other examples of characters finding their moral compasses are portrayed on these programs.

We will explore this in two ways – large scale and small scale. Large scale looks at the battle between good and evil, while small scale looks at things like following rules, exercising control, altruism, and testing the limits. When characters do bad things, what are the consequences?

Because these shows are sitcoms, many of the "situations" that are presented in episodes focus on choices the characters make, the consequences of those choices, and a lesson learned. For example, on *Sabrina the Teenage Witch*, when Sabrina first gets her powers in Season 1, she regularly tries to use them to help herself out of "typical" teenage problems, such as being embarrassed by Libby, the mean girl at school, or finding the perfect date to the school dance, battling rumors, and school being boring. In each instance, when Sabrina tries to "help," the problem becomes exacerbated, and Sabrina has to work together with her aunts to fix it. She transforms Libby into a pineapple; she creates a perfect date out of "man-dough" and causes problems at the school dance; she gives the entire school "truth sprinkles" and some truths hurt her classmates and teachers; and the spell she uses to make school more exciting turns the school into a literal Soap Opera. In these – and almost all – cases, Sabrina learns that she shouldn't use magic to take the easy way out, and that all actions have unforeseen consequences.

Similarly, on *Wizards of Waverly Place*, Alex regularly uses her magic to try to tweak the circumstances, which typically backfires. In the series premiere, Alex learns a duplicating spell and then uses it to make a copy of herself. Her father told her she was not allowed to miss her wizarding lessons, but she wants to go to a super-rare sale at her favorite store. She defies her father by creating her own doppelganger and it backfires on her. Her twin causes chaos – she doesn't end up getting the jacket she wanted anyway, and her father is disappointed in her. Alex and Sabrina are just two of the protagonists on these shows who continuously test the limits. All of the teens do this frequently. As mentioned before, if there were not situations to get in and out of, there would not be sitcoms! Because of this, it is more important to look at the long-term character progression of certain characters to discover the morality lessons incorporated into these programs. We will look at four characters in particular: Violet from *Ultra-Violet & Black Scorpion*, Alex from *Wizards of Waverly Place*, Max from *The Thundermans*, and Amy from *Villains of Valley View*.

Violet is the youngest of the central superheroes on these programs. At 13, she is still in middle school when she is chosen by the luchador mask that makes her Ultra-Violet. Since this show launched in 2022, and was not picked up for a second season, we only have one season to explore Violet's character arc, especially in relation to morality. There are a few ways that we see Violet struggle with her moral compass, and both connect to her sense of self and power. When Violet first becomes Ultra-Violet, she wants to use her newfound superherodom to increase her social media following. She is a digital native and as such she is used to sharing her life online. Her mentor and uncle, Cruz/Black Scorpion, suggests she does not want to "do the work" involved with being a superhero, but wants all the glory and rewards, and he is right. Violet scoffs at workouts and lessons and just wants to go out and fight the "bad guys." When she tries to take on these bad guys on her own, she gets herself into trouble that Black Scorpion has to get her out of. She learns that it is important that she put in the work. She needs to learn. Still, she is tempted to unmask herself so that everyone can know that she is the one behind the mask. Uncle Cruz tries to explain to her that to be a superhero you have to be selfless; that it cannot be about you, it has to be about those you are helping. He is teaching her altruism, but at first Violet does not understand. She is used to being overlooked by her family because of her overachieving older brother who is good at everything. Finally, she is good at something, and she wants the world – and her family – to know! She ultimately experiences the feeling of true altruism in Episode 2, when she rescues a young girl who was lost from her mother. She realizes first-hand that helping people is more fulfilling than any followers and likes on social media. She accepts that it is her responsibility as a superhero to keep her identity hidden. She has internalized this through her actions, not just through listening to her mentor.

Now that she wants to keep her identity secret, she is tested again throughout the season, when she becomes consumed with a classmate blogging about Ultra-Violet. A fellow student is writing a gossip blog, and he is not a fan of Ultra-Violet. Violet is both concerned about being exposed and upset that this person doesn't like Ultra-Violet. When she suggests to her uncle that she use his password cracking device to figure out who the gossip blogger is, he denies her, telling her that it is not a crime to blog, and that they should only use their powers to fight crime. Violet defies Cruz and steals the device. She learns that the blogger is her classmate, Luis. She further uses her power to try to force Luis to stop blogging. It continuously backfires on Violet. The more she tries, the more negative things he writes. She even tries to "show" him some excitement by taking him for a ride with her super-speed. But rather than impressing him, it goads him even more; now he is driven to find out who is behind the Ultra-Violet mask. Violet learns to let it go and accept that not everyone is going to like her. Still, it is a reoccurring character trait that pops up during the season. She wants everyone to like her and tries too hard. This will be discussed further in the chapter on friendship.

The final way that Violet struggles with her moral compass involves the character of Cascada. Cascada is another masked superhero, and unlike Black Scorpion, she believes it is okay to break the rules to help those in need. Violet defies Cruz again by going to a fundraiser with Cascada. Cruz did not want her to use her superhero status for celebrity. Ultra-Violet helps raise a lot of money for the charity, so Violet is conflicted. She did a good thing, but she also defied her uncle and lied to her family. Her internal struggle continues as she starts secretly training with Cascada, who lets her stay up late and take more risks than Black Scorpion. She learns from this as well when Cascada puts her in a situation that she really can't handle alone. Then, Violet figures out that Cascada is really Catalina, her school counselor and Cruz's new girlfriend. Violet begins to suffer from anxiety and has horrible nightmares for keeping this secret from her uncle. She ends up "doing the right thing" and telling her uncle. This shows that Violet values family more than anything else – a theme that is seen consistently in these programs.

As mentioned earlier in this chapter, the *Wizards of Waverly Place*'s Alex Russo tests the limits – of both her parents AND her magic. Like Violet, Alex feels that her family is prouder of her older brother (Justin) than they are of her. This feeling comes to a head during the final two episodes of the series. In the penultimate episode, the three Russo siblings finally compete in their Family Wizard Competition. There are multiple rounds in the competition, and in the final round the three siblings enter a labyrinth. Justin makes it out first and is declared the family wizard; however, he says he can't accept it because Alex should have made it out first, but she came back to help Justin, whose foot was stuck in a tree root. So, Alex becomes the family wizard. Even though Alex finally learned to "do the right thing" and helped her family member rather than winning, she still questions herself and her worthiness.

In the 1-hour special final episode "The Wizards Return: Alex vs. Alex" she continues to struggle with her family's expectations. When she uses her magic to have a personal drive-in movie for her and her best friend, Hartley, her father berates her, "What you did was wrong and unbelievably selfish … now that you're the family wizard it's time to stop using magic for selfish reasons." Her boyfriend, Mason, also accuses her of being selfish when she uses her magic to change the food in a picnic he made for her. She decides to use her magic to try to "smooth out her rough spots" so that her loved ones can accept and appreciate her. She enchants, "Selfish, mean and tired of rejection, take these parts to a place of reflection." The selfish and mean parts of Alex are removed and live in a magic mirror and the remaining Alex is "nice" and "good." The magic mirror shatters and now there are two Alex's – "good" and "evil." Evil Alex teams up with an evil wizard and ends up imprisoning Alex's parents, brother, boyfriend, and best friend. Good Alex battles her evil self and the evil wizard, but they are too strong. Good Alex uses a spell that takes away her powers forever, in order to erase Bad Alex from existence. Bad Alex incorporates back into Good Alex and she is back to her original self, but without magic. Even without magic, now that she is whole, she is able to beat the evil wizard and save her loved ones. She pleads her case to the Crystals of Justice to let her have her powers back, and they first reject her request. After her father suggests, "Please I've been trying to help her grow up. Just give her another chance to change." Alex rebukes them all, "No. I'm sick of everyone telling me to grow up or to change. There is only one person who accepts me for who I am, my best friend Harper. She is my magic." The crystals are swayed by her speech and give her another chance to be the family wizard. Alex has realized that it's both her good qualities and her not-so-likeable qualities that make her the wizard she is, and she is happy with that. When an older relative asks her to give advice to two young family wizards in training she says,

> There's going to be a lot of work ahead of you, and it won't really be easy. And one day only one of you will get to become the family wizard, but until then the most important thing to remember is: Have as much ridiculous fun with magic as you can!

Alex followed her AIC and everything turned out okay. She realized it is okay to not be perfect and to make mistakes.

Another character who struggles with the pressure of family expectations is Max Thunderman from *The Thundermans*. When we meet The Thundermans, we quickly learn that Max is different from the rest of his family. Rather than a superhero, Max wants to be a supervillain. His family is aware of this desire and accept it for the most part. They've allowed him to build an evil lair in the basement which he stocks with a number of gadgets he plans to use for nefarious purposes. Since they are in hiding and not able to use their powers in public, the family is not overly concerned with what they hope to be a phase. Max lives in his evil lair with his pet rabbit, Dr. Colloso, who is being punished and forced to live as an animal. Still, he can talk, so he acts as a pseudo-mentor to Max.

One of the reasons Max says he wants to be a villain is because it is cool. He explains, "You get cool costumes, awesome hideouts, and goatees, it's a lot of fun." But the main reason he wants to be a villain is to differentiate himself from his twin sister, Phoebe. As twins, Max and Phoebe share the same superpowers – telekinesis, freeze breath, and heat breath. In Season 1, Episode 2, Phoebe and Max engage in a prank war that gets increasingly more hostile. At the climax of this prank war, when they've created a situation in which they literally think they have 60 seconds to live, Phoebe asks Max, "Is this super-villain thing really worth it?" He admits, "… maybe not." Phoebe counters, "Then why, Max? Why all this supervillain stuff? You're in a family of superheroes." He retorts,

> Exactly. How else am I going to stand out? Look at you. You've always been so great at being good. Everybody thinks you're going to be like one of the best superheroes ever one day … so what were my choices? Be second best at being good, or be the best at being bad?

Phoebe responds, "I'm glad you shared that with me. Too bad its 30 seconds before we are blown to bits!" But they don't get blown up, of course. Phoebe saves them, and this sets up the conceit for the first three seasons – Max battles within himself – is he a villain or a superhero? Over the course of those three seasons, Max does some selfish and bad things, like using his sister's laser vision to carve his initials into the moon, but the majority of the things are benign and get resolved over the course of an episode.

However, the stakes are raised during the two-part season-finale of Season 3. Max is recruited to become a full-supervillain by Dark Mayhem, the world's most powerful and dangerous supervillain. He shows Max the world's first power-sapping orb and asks him to use it to take ThunderGirl's (Phoebe's) powers. Max is hesitant about the idea, but Dark Mayhem persuades Max to do it in order to prove that he's worth becoming a supervillain. He tells Max to stop living in his sister's shadow. Since we know that it is Max's weakness coming in second to Phoebe, he acquiesces.

First Max uses the orb to take away the rest of his family's power. He then uses his freeze breath to prevent them from escaping and warning Phoebe. As he goes to leave, his dad tells him, "If you go down this path, you are no longer our son." He answers, "Exactly – I'm a supervillain now." When he goes to take away Phoebe's powers at prom, they battle and Phoebe implores him not to seal his fate as a supervillain. She beseeches him,

"Is that really what you want Max? To lose everything? Your friends? Allison [his girlfriend]? Your family?" Dark Mayhem commands him to act, "What are you waiting for, Max. You're this close to having it all!" Max looks around at his friends, his girlfriend, and his family, and responds with tears in his eyes, "I already do." He then restores his family's powers. After the family battles and defeats Dark Mayhem together, Max apologizes to Phoebe. His mom laments "I can't believe my baby is finally a superhero…too bad we have to put you in supervillain prison for helping out Dark Mayhem … just kidding!" All is forgiven.

The final season of *The Thundermans* focuses on Max adjusting to now being a superhero after spending so long trying to be a villain. Phoebe helps him on his journey and they end up teaming up to save their town of Hiddenville. They learn that they have a special twin power that makes them stronger together then as separate superheroes. (This will be discussed further in the chapter on siblings.) In looking at Max's character arc throughout the series, he is the epitome of a developing character, who has learned from his mistakes. His journey to finding his AIC was long and twisted, but he did become a true hero in the end. He realized that he didn't have to compare himself to his sister, and that if he worked WITH his family, he was more powerful than he ever previously thought.

The last character progression to discuss begins her journey where Max Thunderman originally wanted to be. She IS a supervillain. When we meet Amy Madden in the first episode of *The Villains of Valley View* we learn that she is really a supervillain named Havoc who is hiding from the head of all supervillains. She lives in Valley View Texas with her parents and two brothers. The Maddens live next door to their landlady, Celia and her granddaughter, Hartley. Hartley is about as different from Amy than you could ever imagine. She is a member of The Sunshine Club and she is full of smiles and cheer. Despite herself, Amy ends up becoming friends with Hartley, and after Hartley discovers the Madden's secret, she takes it upon herself to teach Amy how to be "normal."

Amy's brother Jake took to being good quickly. In fact, he was inspired to be good even before the Maddens moved to Valley View. He was rescued by Amy/Havoc's archnemesis Starling while out "villain-ing" and her selflessness inspired Jake to be a better person. He embraces life in Valley View. He loves going to school, and is even nominated for Student-of-the-Month. This disappoints the rest of his family. They are holding on to being bad. But slowly, with the help of Hartley, they begin to learn the benefits of leading a non-villainous life. But it takes some time.

Hartley discovers the family secret during the first episode. In the second episode, the family is afraid that Hartley is going to reveal their secret and set out to blackmail her. They can't really understand that Hartley wouldn't expose them because they aren't used to people being trustworthy and nice. At this early point in the season, they really don't comprehend good behavior. They don't understand that keeping your word is a part of being a good friend. This is Hartley's first morality lesson for Amy.

By Episode 6, Amy is learning to be a bit more positive and has developed a close friendship with Hartley. But she is still harboring some of her villainous ways. When Hartley babysits a young girl, Scarlett, who's infatuated with Havoc, Amy jumps at the chance to connect with her. When she sees this Scarlett emulating the worst parts of Havoc/Amy, she is disappointed in both Scarlett and herself. Scarlett wants to live a life with no rules, which was Havoc's claim to fame. Scarlett treats Hartley poorly, and this really bothers Amy. Amy has a heart-to-heart with Scarlett and tells her "Your bad behavior has consequences." Scarlett asks Amy, "Why does Havoc do bad things if they have consequences." Amy seriously ponders this and responds, "Maybe she never thought about them." As Scarlett considers this, she then tells Amy, "Just so you know I don't only like Havoc because she doesn't follow the rules. She is strong and doesn't care what people think and always stands up for herself." Amy smiles and suggests, "Why not take some of Havoc's qualities and mix them with Hartley's?" While Amy is teaching Scarlett, she is also giving herself the same advice. She is beginning to think about the consequences of her actions. She is developing empathy by thinking about Hartley's feelings in the situation. Amy began the season in Kohlberg's first level of moral reasoning, and she has now moved into the second level.

Still, like Alex on *Wizards of Waverly Place*, Amy is not going to change her core personality. She will always have a bit of Havoc in her. Because of her new-found empathy, Amy gets mad when Hartley's frenemy, Gem, humiliates Hartley during a singing audition. Amy uses her sonic powers to sabotage Gem's callback audition. Amy expects Hartley to be happy, but she is upset. She explains to Amy that her behavior makes her feel that Amy doesn't think she can handle things on her own. This is yet another morality lesson that Hartley impresses on Amy, but in a more indirect way. Amy learns that she can't just resort to using her powers to solve problems, and that sometimes there is not an easy solution or fix. In the end of that specific episode, Amy and Hartley decide to form their own singing group, and the first song they write and sing together describes the balanced duality of their friendship. Amy sings "Won't lie. I tried to be sugar sweet but I'm not a saint. Won't lie. Sometimes I'm running wild but sometimes I ain't." Then Hartley joins in, "Won't lie. Don't mind, because nothing ever stays the same." Together they harmonize,

> I'm not living perfectly. No. But I don't wanna be. I wanna wake up, take the good with all the bad. I wanna run, fly, laugh, cry, never looking back. What good is day without the night? What good is dark without the light? Just like the sunrise, the best part's gonna be somewhere in between.

They appreciate each other for who they are.

By the final episode of the first season of *The Villains of Valley View*, the Madden family come full circle and begin to embrace their life in Valley View. When they are forced to return to their old home in Metropolis to rescue Amy's brother Colby, they reflect that it no longer feels like home there and that they miss Texas. When villain Oculus tells Hartley, "You really believe Havoc is your friend? She's a villain." Harley retorts "You're wrong. When Havoc became Amy she changed. They've all changed."

Time will tell if Amy has fully changed, since in the season finale Amy defeats the head of all supervillains, Onyx. Just as the family is about to return to Valley View, another villain tells Amy, "Now that you've beaten Onyx, YOU are the head of all supervillains." *The Villains of Valley View* was renewed for a second season, and that season will likely continue Amy's journey to find her AIC. Will she stay good, or be tempted by the "dark side"? No matter what Amy decides to do, one thing is certain: Hartley will be by her side.

Friendships like Amy's and Hartley's are a crucial ingredient of adolescence. Chapter 6 will discuss the importance of friendship and how they are portrayed in secret-identity tween sitcoms in more detail.

References

Assor, Avi. 2012. "Allowing choice and nurturing an inner compass: Educational practices supporting students' need for autonomy." In Christenson, S. Reschly, A. and Wylie, C. (eds.) *Handbook of research on student engagement*. 421–439. Boston, MA.

Deci, Edward and Ryan, Richard 1985. *Intrinsic Motivation and Self-Determination in Human Behavior*. New York: Plenum.

Kohlberg, Lawrence. 1981. *The Philosophy of Moral Development: Moral Stages and the Idea of Justice*. San Francisco: Harper & Row.

6 Friendships

Chapter 2 introduced Erikson's Stages of Psychosocial Development, a theory from 1950 that outlines key psychological strengths, or virtues, that develop at different stages of life. Erikson describes each stage as having a "dominant crisis" or challenge that people typically face. According to him, the main goal in each stage is to find a healthy balance between the two sides of this crisis, which helps people develop specific virtues. These eight stages cover the entire lifespan, from birth to death. However, the stages most relevant to this book's topic are Stages IV and V.

Stage IV typically occurs between the ages of 7 and 12 (which is the age of many viewers of secret-identity tween shows). The crisis present in this stage is "industry versus inferiority." Industry involves a child learning to be productive and accept evaluation of his or her efforts. Inferiority describes a child being unproductive, discouraged in their efforts, and feeling incompetent and substandard. In this stage, children are moving out of a more "playful" stage and start taming their imagination and dedicating themselves to education and learning the social skills that society requires of them. No longer are parents the only social influences. They are also influenced by teachers, peers, and community members. Erikson describes a healthy balance of industry and inferiority as exhibiting the virtue of *competency*: mostly industry with just a touch of inferiority to keep us sensibly humble (Erikson 1950).

Erikson's fifth stage coincides with adolescence and begins with puberty and ends between around age 18 to 20. While most of the viewers of these tween programs would not be at this later end of the age spectrum, some of the characters on these programs do reach the end of this stage by the completion of the full run of the show. The crisis in this period is "ego-identity versus role-confusion." Erikson explains that ego-identity means knowing who you are and how you fit into the rest of society. It requires that you take all you've learned about life and yourself and mold it into a unified self-image, one that your community finds meaningful. Role-confusion would involve uncertainty about a given social or group role. If you successfully negotiate this stage, you will have

DOI: 10.4324/9781003593027-6

the virtue Erikson called *fidelity*. Fidelity means loyalty, the ability to live by societies' standards despite their imperfections and incompleteness and inconsistencies. You may still question those standards and imperfections, but fidelity means that you have found a place in that community, a place that will allow you to contribute (Erikson 1950).

Erikson also identifies key relationships that have significant meaning during each stage. During Stage IV, the significant relationship is neighborhood and school. In Stage V, it is peer groups and role models. Friendships are very influential during these stages and build a foundation for interpersonal relationships later in life. There is a plethora of research that cites the importance of friendships during adolescence (for a review see Youniss and Haynie 1992). These relationships provide environments for acquiring social support, learning interpersonal skills, developing social competence, and gathering information for self-knowledge and esteem (Parker and Asher, 1993; Hartup, 1989). Early adolescence is an especially important developmental period to consider, in part, because friends are a major socialization agent during this life stage (Parker and Asher, 1993; Hartup, 1989). According to Csikszentmihalyi & Larson (1984) adolescents spend twice as much time with their friends as with their parents, siblings, and other adults – even outside of the classroom.

Savin-Williams and Berndt (1990) explain young people feel understood by their friends and can totally be themselves with them. They reviewed literature on adolescent friendships and found correlations that suggest young people with close supportive friendship have higher self-esteem, understand other people's feelings better, behave better in school, and do better academically.

Adolescent friendships are typically characterized by similarity interests and values, self-disclosure, and support. Close friendships tend to begin even earlier than the onset of puberty. According to Levine and Munsch (2011),

> Children between the ages of 6 and 12 begin to value having a "best friend" and this friendship is more likely to be marked by a commitment to each other based on trust. Friends spend time together, like to do the same kinds of things, and increasingly offer each other emotional support. However, friendships will vary in the amount of loyalty and commitment, self-disclosure, and conflict they contain.
>
> (Levine and Munsch 2011, 441)

Self-disclosure is both a risk and a benefit to any interpersonal relationship, including friendships. It is necessary to form the bonds of friendship, but it leaves a person vulnerable to betrayal. This is a dominant theme of friendship seen in these double-identity tween programs. Trust is a hallmark of adolescent friendships and, as will be discussed later in this chapter, occupies a bulk of character interplay on these shows. The risks of self-disclosure in "real life" are amplified in "reel life." In reality, if a tween confesses a secret to a friend and that friend divulges their secret, it could cause humiliation and embarrassment, and may lead to conflict; but in the world of secret lives, if a character confides their secret identity to a friend, and that friend betrays their trust, it could have much bigger implications. A whole wizarding or superhero world may be exposed and be at risk of annihilation. If a spy's identity is exposed by her friend, her very life may be in danger. This amplification of the importance of trust emphasizes just how valuable loyalty and trust is in adolescent and tween friendships.

The remainder of this chapter will explore the portrayal of trust and other aspects of friendships on these secret-identity tween sitcoms. For almost all of the programs (except *Lab Rats* and *Lab Rats: Elite Force*), the protagonist (or one of the main protagonists) has one or two close friends for the duration of the show. These programs will be discussed, from our earliest program (*Sabrina the Teenage Witch*) to the most recent (*Ultra-Violet & Black Scorpion*) to better understand the model of friendship being portrayed to tween viewers of these programs.

Friendship on *Sabrina the Teenage Witch*

Sabrina Spellman moves in with her aunts when she turns 16 and learns she is a witch. To add to all of this change, she also starts attending a new high school. On her first day, Sabrina meets Jenny Kelley and they become fast friends. Sabrina and Jenny spend time together both in and out of school. They have each other's backs when mean-girl Libby torments them. They both befriend Harvey Kinkle, and for one episode it seems that they both like him as "more than a friend." They both decide that they don't want to ruin their friendship, but then Sabrina tries to do what she thinks is the right thing and tells Jenny to ask Harvey out. She does and discovers they have nothing in common. Sabrina and Harvey then end up dating, and Jenny is happy for them. In Season 1 Episode 13 "Jenny's Non-Dream" Jenny wonders why Sabrina never invites her over to her house. So, Sabrina decides to have her over for a slumber party. Sabrina and her aunts do their best to keep their magic hidden while Jenny is there, but she accidentally stumbles into the Other Realm through the linen closet. Due to the rules of the Other Realm, she gets turned into a grasshopper. Sabrina finds a loophole in the rules: mortals with no conscious knowledge of the Other Realm can pass through safely. So, they convince Jenny that she is having a dream, so that she does not have "conscious" knowledge. Sabrina never tells Jenny her secret, and while they do hang out often, there are not many friend-centric episodes after this one during the first season. When the show is renewed and comes back for a second season, it seems that Jenny has moved out of town.

At the beginning of the second season, Sabrina starts back to school on her 17th birthday and meets a new student, Valerie. Sabrina takes Valerie under her wing and they become friends. Valerie takes over Jenny's job as fellow "Libby-hater" and Sabrina's sidekick.

Valerie is a regular part of Sabrina's life for the rest of Seasons 2 and 3, but at the start of the fourth season Valerie moves with her family to Alaska. The relationship that lasts the longest for Sabrina, and received the most attention, is with her boyfriend, Harvey, rather than a friend. This relationship will be discussed further in Chapter 7. Still, there is one episode that illustrates Sabrina's relationship with both Harvey and Valerie. On the 10th episode of Season 2, Sabrina learns that she can tell mortals her secret and they will forget at midnight, because it is Friday the 13th. Her aunts warn her about the bad consequences that could occur if she chooses to tell anyone, but Sabrina decides to tell Valerie and Harvey. She is confident she can trust Valerie and Harvey, so she tells them she is a witch. They are not fazed by Sabrina's news. They accept that she is a witch and they spend the day in the Other Realm and cast various spells. Mean-girl Libby overhears Sabrina's confession and tells the media and the PTA. When Libby tries to have Valerie and Harvey corroborate what she heard, they protect Sabrina and lie to the crowd. They prove that they are trustworthy friends.

Friendship on *Hannah Montana*

The conflict of Miley Stewart's friends not knowing she is Hannah Montana is set up from the very beginning of the show. Episode 1 is centered on Miley trying to keep her secret from her best friend, Lilly, and the second episode involves attempting to further keep it from her close friend, Oliver. Since these are early episodes, they are also introducing us to what Miley's life is like as Hannah Montana. Lilly and Oliver are superfans of Hannah Montana; in fact, Oliver is a bit obsessed with her. Lilly gets two tickets to the Hannah Montana concert and invites Miley to join her. That will be a little hard to do, since Miley will be on stage as Hannah. But as a situational comedy, this provides an opportunity to see Miley try to juggle both her identities. Before she puts herself in this impossible position, her father advises Miley to consider telling Lilly the truth. He tells her, "I know you're concerned that if Lilly finds out she won't treat you the same. But she's still your best bud. You need to trust that." But Miley isn't ready to reveal her secret. So, she doesn't tell Lilly; instead Lilly discovers it on her own at the concert. When she goes to visit Hannah Montana in her dressing room, she sees the bracelet she gave to Miley on Hannah's wrist and puts two and two together. Lilly is disappointed that Miley didn't think she could tell Lilly the secret. Hannah defends herself by explaining, "Maybe once you knew, you wouldn't want to be my friend. Maybe you'd like

Hannah Montana more than me. Everything that I was afraid happened, happened. Now it's ruined everything." Lilly forgives her and reassures her, "You're the one I want to talk to – not Hannah Montana."

Even after telling Lilly, she still doesn't want to share her secret with Oliver, because he is so fixated on Hannah Montana. So instead, she devises a plan to try to get Oliver to think that Hannah Montana is a jerk, so he doesn't like her. She interacts with him as Hannah and treats him rudely, but he does not give up. Even after she starts chawing a huge mouthful of gum (which Miley knows is his biggest pet peeve), he won't stop thinking that Hannah Montana is his dream girl. Finally, Hannah/Miley yells at him, "What does it take for you to understand. You and Hannah Montana are NEVER going to be together!" Oliver asks, "Why not?" Hannah takes off her wig to reveal herself, saying "Because I am Hannah Montana. Me. Miley." They end up laughing about it after discussing that the girl Oliver THOUGHT he was in love with all this time was actually his friend, and he didn't love her. Miley asks, "So what do you think, are we going to be okay." Oliver assures her, "Yeah, we're okay." Many times on Hannah Montana, Hannah's songs reveal her inner thoughts on situations. In this episode, she sings,

> "This is the life. And I'm still getting it right." "So what you see is only half the story – there's another side of me.....I'm a lucky girl whose dreams came true. But underneath it all I'm just like you."

During the four seasons of the show, Lilly and Oliver never divulge her secret. In fact, Lilly actually creates her own secret identity as Lola LaFonda, so that she can be with Miley when she's "being" Hannah.

In the final season of the show, Miley starts to question if she wants to continue with her double life and finally reveals herself so she can live life as Miley (this will be discussed further in the final chapter). In the final episodes, Lilly and Miley were supposed to go to college and then Miley ends up getting a movie offer in Paris, and Lilly is extremely upset at Miley for not telling her and then not asking her to go with her to Paris. As she explains to Miley, "I need to know that this friendship is as important to you as it does to me." At first Lilly decides to put off college to go to Paris with Miley. But then she realizes that there will always be a concert or a movie offer and she doesn't want to miss having her own experiences at college. Miley and Lilly go their separate ways, but in Paris, Miley has a change of heart. During a musical montage she reflects as we hear her lyrics:

> I always knew this day would come
> We'd be standing one by one
> With our future in our hands
> So many dreams, so many plans

I always knew after all these years
There'd be laughter, there'd be tears
But never thought I'd walk away
With so much joy, but so much pain
And it's so hard to say "goodbye"
But yesterday's gone
We gotta keep moving on
I'm so thankful for the moments
So glad I got to know you
The times that we had
I'll keep like a photograph
And hold you in my heart forever
I'll always remember you
Another chapter in the book
Can't go back, but you can look
And there we are on every page
Memories I'll always save
Up ahead on the open doors
Who knows what we're heading towards?
I wish you love, I wish you luck
For you, the world just opens up
But it's so hard to say "goodbye"
Yesterday's gone
We gotta keep moving on
I'm so thankful for the moments
So glad I got to know you
The times that we had
I'll keep like a photograph
And hold you in my heart forever
I'll always remember you
Everyday that we had
All the good, all the bad
I'll keep 'em here inside
All the times that we shared
Every place, everywhere
You touched my life
Yeah, one day, we'll look back
We'll smile and we'll laugh
But right now we just cry
'Cause it's so hard to say "goodbye"
Yesterday's gone
We gotta keep moving on
I'm so thankful for the moments
So glad I got to know you

The times that we had
I'll keep like a photograph
And hold you in my heart forever
I'll always remember you
I'll always remember you
Yeah, hey, yeah, yeah
I'll always remember you

Songwriters: Allan Mitch / Jesse Leigh Alexander
I'll Always Remember You lyrics © Walt Disney
Music Company, Happy Tears Music

In the last scene of the series, we see Lilly alone in her dorm room reading a textbook and she hears a knock at the door. It's Miley wearing a Stanford sweatshirt and she says, "I'm Miley. I'm your new roommate." She explains to Lilly, "You were right. There's gonna be a million concerts and tours and movies, but I only get one chance to go to college with my best friend. I love you so much." Lilly responds, "I know!" Lilly knows that she is more important to Miley than the fame and the life of a pop star. When the show began, Miley just wanted to live a normal life. By the end, she realizes her life will never be normal, but it doesn't matter if she has Lilly by her side.

Friendship on *Wizards of Waverly Place*

In *Wizards of Waverly Place*, Alex's best friend is Harper Finkle. The previous chapter discussed Alex and Harper when looking at Alex's journey to her AIC. To briefly review, in the final episode of the series, Alex realizes that the only person in her life that doesn't want her to grow up and change who she is, is Harper. She tells the Crystals of Justice, "My best friend Harper is my magic." This culmination of the show perfectly reflects Alex and Harper's relationship throughout the entire series.

Alex and Harper have been friends since kindergarten, but she doesn't find out that Alex is a wizard until the second season of the show. Harper gets mad at Alex for forgetting her birthday again and lying to her about going to PopCon. Alex didn't really lie, but she can't tell Harper the truth, because it will reveal her secret. After a series of events, Harper thinks that Alex setup a birthday surprise and literally says, "Thank you for telling me the truth. You are the best friend ever." Alex knows she is not telling the truth, and it makes her feel like a horrible friend, so she explains what really happened and tells her, "I'm a wizard." Harper does not believe her, so Alex uses her magic to take Harper to space and conjures a birthday cupcake. Harper exclaims, "I'm eating a birthday cupcake in space with my best friend who is a wizard!"

From that point on, Harper becomes involved in the Russo's magical mayhem. In Episode 16 of Season 2, "Future Harper" we learn that in the future, Harper writes about her wizarding adventures with the Russos in a series of books. After CURRENT Harper predicts the end of a story Alex is recounting, and tells her it was from a new book she just read, Justin Russo reads the book – and all the books by author H.J. Darling and discovers that all of the stories are actual events that they've encountered. The Russo siblings track down the author, H.J. Darling, and find that she is actually an adult Harper. Adult Harper reveals that she couldn't write these stories in the future because by then the wizarding world has been exposed, and so the stories aren't as magical and marketable. Therefore, she has traveled back in time with the help of a very powerful wizard (Is it Justin? Is it Alex? Is it Max?) to publish the stories in the present/past. At first Alex is mad at Future Harper that she used her stories without her permission. She transfers her anger to Current Harper, who has no idea why Alex is mad at her. Justin convinces Alex, who doesn't like to read, to read the books so she can see how they are all about the adventures of Alex and Harper. She reads the books and enjoys them and convinces Current Harper that she should write about their adventures in the future. During their discussion, Alex tells Harper, "I just hope that we're friends for a really long time." Harper replies, "Alex, is that what you are afraid of? That we wouldn't be friends?" Alex confesses, "Well, I was afraid of that, but not anymore. I'm pretty sure we're going to be friends forever."

Friendship on *Mighty Med*

The core friendship seen on *Mighty Med* is that of Kaz and Oliver. As the main characters of the program, the entire series is focused on them and their adventures together at the hospital for superheroes where they work. Kaz and Oliver have been best friends their entire lives, and they always have the other's back. Their friendship can be summed up by a specific exchange during Season 1, Episode 6 "Pranks for Nothing." First, we get insight to the duration of their friendship when Oliver tells Kaz, "I've been pranking you since before you were born." Kaz responds, "Oliver, you're three days older than me." Oliver retorts, "I know. I came out sideways just to mess with my mom." Later in the episode, we fully understand the depth of their friendship. The pranks have gotten out of hand, and they *believe* they are hurtling to space and might die. Oliver articulates his feelings for his best friend, "Now listen, if these are our last minutes alive, I'm glad I'm spending them with you." Kaz agrees, "Me too, man. You're the best friend I could ever have. I love you." The sentimental moment doesn't last more than a minute, however, when Dr. Diaz and Skylar Storm mock them for being sappy and tell them the danger was all a prank. But, whether the dangerous situation was real or not, the audience knows that the feelings behind Oliver's and Kaz's exchange were genuine.

Friendship on *The Thundermans*

The friendship that is central to *The Thundermans* is that of Phoebe Thunderman and Cherry Seinfeld. As Phoebe adjusts to living as a normal teenager in Hiddenville, she is excited to make a new friend, Cherry. Even though her parents have a rule about having people over to the house, to make sure they don't uncover their secret, Phoebe invites Cherry over to help her babysit her younger siblings. Phoebe accidently levitates her siblings with her telekinesis. When she sees Cherry's shocked face, she panics and uses her freeze breath to freeze her. She then concocts a plan to make it look like Billy and Nora were practicing for a play and that they were actually hoisted into the air by ropes. It's a close call, and Phoebe will continue to keep her true identity hidden from Cherry for the remainder of the first season and most of the second season. In the Season 2 finale, Phoebe's mom has a baby – in fast superhero fashion – and Phoebe has to abandon Cherry on a double-date. Cherry is furious and comes over to the Thunderman house to confront Phoebe. She discovers Phoebe's new baby sister and questions Phoebe, "You have a new baby sister and you didn't tell me?" Phoebe pretends to talk as baby Chloe and responds, "Don't be mad at Phoebe. You guys are friends." Cherry probes Phoebe, "Are we? Honestly, I feel like you're always hiding things from me." Phoebe answers her, "I know. The truth is I do have a lot of secrets. I just can't tell you any of them." Cherry counters, "What kind of best friends don't tell each other everything?" When Phoebe can't answer, Cherry storms off, "I guess that's my answer." But she stays sulking on the Thundermans' porch. Right after this, Phoebe learns her brother Max is in trouble and she is the only one who can rescue him – but, she is still babysitting her new baby sister. She runs out to Cherry on the porch to ask her to watch Chloe. But then as she is about to be driven away in the Thundervan, Phoebe stops and tells Cherry to get in with the baby. As they drive away, Chloe asks, "Uh, how is this van driving itself?" Phoebe responds, "Cherry, have you ever heard of Thunderman?" Once Phoebe tells Cherry everything, Cherry does not believe her at all. She still thinks Phoebe is telling lies. While Cherry is feeding the baby, she has a superhero growth spurt and becomes a toddler. Cherry goes to find Phoebe and witnesses her doing her superhero thing to rescue Max. When the dust settles Cherry apologizes for not believing her and promises to keep the family secret. She keeps her word for the remainder of the series.

However, in Season 3 Episode 19, the Hero League forces Phoebe to end her friendship with Cherry after Cherry takes a selfie with Phoebe for the Best of Besties contest that exposes the Thundermans portrait in its background. Phoebe is unable to tell Cherry that they can't hang out anymore because she doesn't want to lose the friendship. When Cherry disappears, Phoebe searches for her and discovers that she was taken by the Hero League to get her memory wiped. Phoebe goes to rescue her and pleads with the head of the Hero League, President Kickbutt, "Cherry is the best thing that happened to me since moving to Hiddenville. If I have to sacrifice being a superhero to keep you from wiping her memory, I will." President Kickbutt clears things up, "We weren't going to wipe her memory, we were going to wipe her PHONE'S memory." Cherry thanks Phoebe for being willing to sacrifice her powers for their friendship. They lament that it doesn't matter if they don't win the Best of the Besties contest at school. Phoebe reminds Cherry, "Who cares what the kids at school think. We know we're the best of the besties."

Friendship on *Henry Danger*

In *Henry Danger*, Henry Hart has two best friends, Charlotte and Jasper. In the fourth episode of the first season, Charlotte confronts Henry about being Kid Danger. While he tries to deny it, Charlotte keeps pushing; she has figured it out, and she just wants Henry to confirm it. Charlotte had already been working with Henry at Captain Man's "cover" job – the store Junk 'N Stuff. Now that she knows Henry's secret, she gets a job working for Captain Man and Kid Danger as an information assistant. So, from that point on, Charlotte goes to school with Henry, works with both Henry and Kid Danger, and always supports him. It takes almost two full seasons for Henry's other best friend, Jasper, to learn the secret and join his friends fighting crime. In the second season finale, "I Know Your Secret" Henry transforms into Kid Danger in front of Jasper, because he mistakenly believes Jasper had learned his secret. Jasper is totally shocked. Captain Man tells Henry and Charlotte that it is too risky to let anyone else know who they are and that he is going to have to erase Jasper's memory. Henry asks him for a moment with him first. He explains, "We've been friends since we were five." After they talk for a while Jasper says, "You've always been a good friend to me, Kid Danger. I'm proud of you." Henry tells Ray/Captain Man that they can't erase his memory. Captain Man argues that he is too much of a security risk. But Henry persists, "We leave Jasper the way he is or else I can't be Kid Danger anymore … I don't want to quit, but if you're gonna erase all the memories of my oldest friend's brain, then I don't want this anymore." Captain Man backs down and lets Jasper keep his memory. So now Henry is only keeping his secret from his family, not his two best friends. They continue to work together until the end of the series. And even then, when Henry stops working for Captain Man, we learn that Henry, Charlotte, and Jasper are all living in another town, fighting crime as a team.

Friendship on *K.C. Undercover*

From the premiere episode of *K.C. Undercover*, the audience knows that K.C.'s best friend is Marissa Clark. Marisa is very outgoing and fun and balances out K.C.'s more serious nature. She encourages her to have more fun and experience typical high school life. During the premiere episode, Marisa tries to convince K.C. to attend a school dance, but K.C. has a robotics meeting and says she does not want to go. K.C. ends up attending the dance after all, but only because once she agrees to be a spy she needs to attend the dance for a mission. When K.C. calls Marissa to ask her what she should wear to the dance, Marissa is at the door in mere seconds, with two dresses to choose from.

Marissa discovers K.C.'s secret during Season 1 Episode 6 "Photo Bombed." Marissa is mad at K.C. for not letting her enter a picture Marisa took of her into a contest. K.C. can't risk having her photo published because it could risk her cover as an agent. Then she sees K.C. out at a hibachi restaurant and recognizes K.C. in her disguise battling a criminal. K.C. brings Marissa back to her house and explains everything. But, since The Organization has rules about people knowing agents' identities, K.C. is forced to erase Marissa's memory. We witness K.C.'s parents giving her the memory spray, and K.C. explaining the process to Marissa. She tells her that after she gets the spray, she won't remember why K.C. wouldn't let her enter her photo in the contest and might not want to be her friend anymore. She tells Marissa, "And even though you won't like me, I will always love you." Marissa responds, "I will always love you too, K.C. No matter what. Even if I don't know I do." K.C.'s father gets emotional and watches with her mother as she sprays her best friend. Marissa immediately slumps on the couch. When her parents tell her how proud they are of her, she says she understands that Marissa could never know the truth about them. They leave the room and K.C. rouses Marissa, "All clear!" K.C. sprayed fake memory spray. Marissa still knows their secret, and she keeps it for the remainder of the series.

In the series finale, Marissa brings K.C.'s yearbook to her after 2 months. She explains, "I finally signed your yearbook. Better late than never. Check out what I wrote in your yearbook." We see an almost blank page, with "Dear K.C." at the top and "Love, Marissa" at the bottom. K.C. asks her why it's blank and Marissa responds,

> That's where you're wrong, smarty pants. It's not blank, it's ready to be filled in … filled in with our future … If I write something down on that page, that means our stories over and it is not over. It is just starting. And it doesn't matter if we live right next door to each other or across the world. You will always be my best friend.

Friendship on *Ultra-Violet & Black Scorpion*

Violet Rodriguez's best friend is Maya Miller-Martinez. When the series begins, we meet Violet and Maya and get a sense for what their life as like as typical 13-year olds. But Violet's life is about to become anything but typical, when she discovers a magic luchador mask in her bedroom. When she dons the mask her hair turns purple and she discovers she has super-speed. The next thing she does is call Maya over and show her. She even lets her try on the mask, but it does not work for Maya, only Violet.

Because Maya is a digital native, she also immediately wants to share her newfound super-status on social media. So, she asks Maya to film her, creates a social media account for Ultra-Violet, and posts her unbelievable speed.

Since Maya knows about her secret identity from the very beginning, we don't have the "keeping my identity from my best friend" storyline that we had in the other shows. Still, Maya and Violet do have some conflict throughout the first and only season of the program. In Episode 4 "Sleepover Showdown," Maya is invited to a sleepover at another girl's house and Violet is not invited. Maya asks the girl if she can bring Violet, and when she does, Violet tries too hard to impress these new friends. This upsets Maya, and Violet and Maya have their first real fight. Violet tells Maya that she doesn't understand why Maya is mad that she wants these girls to like her. Maya tells Violet, "They don't like you. They like Ultra-Violet." This stings, but Violet knows she is right. They end up having a heart-to-heart. Violet confesses her feelings, "The only thing that's great about me is Ultra-Violet and I can't tell anyone." Maya corrects her, "Ultra-Violet isn't the best thing about you. I liked you from the first day we met in second grade. You were regular old Violet … ." Violet is still feeling a bit dejected. She says, "Well you're the only one, or else I wouldn't have been your pity invite." Maya clarifies, "I invited you because I thought we'd have a good time together and I hardly know these girls. I was nervous to go by myself." They hug and make up.

However, that was not their last conflict. In Episode 11 "Ultra Friend and Ultra Fake" Violet promises to help Maya practice her eSports but misses practice while trying to stop prisoners escaping. When Violet further misses her eSports tournament, Maya becomes upset. When Violet tries to apologize, Maya says,

> I should have known. You always choose Ultra-Violet over me … I am always there for you AND Ultra-Violet. But for some reason, neither of you can be there for me … ever since you've got the mask, you haven't been a very good friend.

Violet pleads, "I said I was sorry, Maya." Maya answers, "Yeah, I know. But sometimes sorry doesn't fix it."

In the next episode, Episode 12 "Forgive Me Not" Violet works to earn Maya's forgiveness and earn back her friendship, but nothing she tries succeeds. She tries tricking her into hanging out by asking their teacher to pair them together for an assignment. Maya sees through this and switches partners with Luis. After witnessing Cruz not giving his ex-girlfriend space, Violet realizes that she too is refusing to respect boundaries. Once she realizes this, she gives Maya the space she needs, and Maya eventually comes around. She explains to Violet,

> We were never NOT friends, I just needed time to think. So much has been changing ever since you became Ultra-Violet. It's great and exciting, but a lot of it is about her. And sometimes I still need it to be about us. And when you missed my event, it really hurt.

Violet tells her she wishes she could turn back time and be there. She promises, "If it ever comes down to you or Ultra-Violet again, I choose you." But Maya tells her, "You don't have to choose. This city needs Ultra-Violet and I like being a part of her adventures."

Friendship on *The Villains of Valley View*

The friendship of Amy and Hartley on *The Villains of Valley View* was introduced in the previous chapter. The examples provided in that chapter described how Hartley teaches Amy to be a better person and how to be a friend. By not exposing The Maddens, Hartley is teaching Amy that "friends don't tell your secrets." Hartley also teaches Amy that "Friends protect their feelings." She does this when her brother Jake starts seeing Amy's nemesis from Metropolis, Starling. Hartley explains that she didn't want Amy to be hurt and upset. Just as Amy and Hartley's first song described how the balance of their personalities made their friendship special, the next song they wrote was about not letting others make them feel bad about themselves. In Season 1 Episode 16 "We Don't Care" Amy and Hartley write a song by that same name for the Battle of the Bands. Some of the lyrics describe how as long as they like themselves, and each other, *they don't care*:

> Amy: No more stopping, only green lights
> No more Mr. Shy Guy
> Won't spend any time
> Trying to be what they like
> If they try to turn it down
> We'll just turn it way up loud

Hartley: Never let the critics faze us
Leave the hate in the dust
Being real is a must
Won't keep it hush-hush
If they try to turn it down,
We'll just turn it way up load

Both: What's the difference if you're different?
Just go with it and make 'em listen

Chorus: We don't care, they can't stop us now
No more hiding back in the crowd
So let 'em say, hey, what they say, hey
We don't, we don't, we don't care
We don't care if we don't fit in
We won't let 'em under out skin
So let 'em say, hey, what they'll say hey
We don't, we don't, we don't care

Hartley: We don't care about the talk, talk
It don't get to us, nah
We do what we want

Amy: We're just having fun, yeah
If they try to turn it down
We'll just turn it way up loud.
Repeats Chorus
Lyrics by Simon Oscroft & Sofia Quinn

Conclusion

The core friendships on each of these secret-identity tween sitcoms emphasize the importance of trust in friendships, through the characters' trust of their best friend with their life-altering secret. With the amplification of the repercussions for breaking a trust for characters of these shows, tween audiences are consistently reminded of the importance of being a loyal friend.

References

Erikson, Erik. 1950. *Childhood and Society*. W.W. Norton & Co.
Hartup, W.W. 1989. "Behavioral Manifestations of Children's Friendships." In T.J. Berndt. & G.W. Ladd (Eds). *Peer Relationships in Child Development*. 46–70. New York: Wiley.

Levine, Laura and Munsch, Joyce. 2011. *Child Development: An Active Learning Approach*. Washington DC: Sage.

Parker, Jeffrey G. and Asher, Steven R. 1993. "Friendship and friendship Quality in Middle Childhood: Links with Peer Group Acceptance and Feelings of Loneliness and Social Dissatisfaction." *Developmental Psychology*, *29* (4) 611–621.

Savin-Williams, R. and Berndt, T.J. 1990. "Friendship and peer relations." In S.S. Felman & G.R. Elliott (Eds.) *At the threshold: The developing adolescent* (pp. 277–307). Cambridge MA: Harvard University Press.

Youniss, James and Haynie, Denise L. 1992. "Friendship in Adolescence." *Developmental and Behavioral Pediatrics*, *13* (1), 59–66.

7 Romance

Just as loyalty and trust are important in friendships, they are also critical ingredients for successful romantic relationships. If we circle back to Erickson's Stages of Psychosocial development, specifically Stages IV and V, we remember that these stages involve developing *competency* and *fidelity* – finding your place in society and living within society's standards. These stages are marked by the movement outside of your familial circle into peer groups and other interpersonal connections. Across adolescence, romantic relationships evolve from engaging in mixed-gender peer groups to group dates in early adolescence (ages 12–14) and from casual dating to exclusive, steady involvement with one partner during mid (ages 15–16) to late (ages 17–19) adolescence (Connolly et al. 2004).

Romantic relationships are related to many of the developmental tasks of adolescence. They play an important role in the development of identity (including sexual identity), influence the process of individuation from the family, change the nature of peer relationships, and lay the groundwork for future intimate relationships (Levine and Munsch, 2011). When reviewing research into adolescent romantic relationships, there is not a set definition about what defines romance. It is not necessarily physical in nature, but rather involves differing levels of emotional intimacy and exclusivity.

As with friendship, the risks of emotional intimacy compete with its benefits. Sharing yourself with another person makes you vulnerable. And, similar to our discussion in the chapter on friendship, those risks are amplified in the lives of teens with secret identities. It is a big risk to tell someone you have feelings for that you are not exactly who you've said you are when you first met. What if they don't like the real you? What if they are mad at you for keeping secrets? Will they be able to forgive you? These revelation repercussions will be discussed later in the chapter when we review the various major romantic partnerships on these shows. But first, let's take a step back and explore the significance of developing

DOI: 10.4324/9781003593027-7

romantic relationships during adolescence. Why is this an important developmental milestone?

Both physical and social changes and expectations that develop during adolescence contribute to this important part of a young person's life. Physically, their bodies are going through puberty, and the hormonal changes begin to signal their bodies' sexual urges. Pairing those physical adjustments with Western society's social norms of dating behavior (Dornsbusch et al. 1987) nurtures the expectation of romantic interests during adolescence. Collins, Welsh, and Furman (2009) provide a very thorough overview of the various theories and concepts related to adolescent romance. But for this discussion we will briefly review two theoretical perspectives that help us understand adolescent romance a little better: the ecological perspective and interpersonal perspective. From the ecological perspective, Larson and Wilson (2004) explain that various social and cultural structures both encourage and constrain romantic relationships during adolescence. These structures include families and peers as well as cultural contexts (which would include ethnicity and religious institutions).

When looking at adolescent romantic relationships through an interpersonal lens, researchers typically explore how the development of romantic relationships, as well as changes in those relationships, contributes to individual development. Researchers such as Laursen and Bukowski (1997) use interdependence models to explore this in more detail. Research typically explores both how early childhood attachments with family and peers influence adolescent romantic relationships, and then conversely how adolescent romantic relationships influence future adult attachments. This follows the basic tenets of Bowlby's Attachment Theory (1958). According to Bowlby, bonding with other humans is an intrinsic human need, and allows us to learn to regulate our emotions, which helps us live longer, healthier lives. Bonding also teaches us to adapt, which encourages both physical and emotional growth. In other words, we need to interact with others to live better lives.

So, when looking at the portrayal of romantic relationships on secret-lives tween TV, it is important to explore the relationships themselves and the benefits and drawbacks they bring to our characters (interpersonal perspective), but also any social structures or cultural contexts that constrain these relationships (ecological perspective).

Given the nature of these programs, the cultural constraints are usually symbolically portrayed. For example, rather than portraying an interracial romantic relationship and any potential implications that may arise from that, these shows instead portray relationships between different magic species. In *Wizards of Waverly Place*, for instance, Alex's longest-lasting romantic relationship is with Mason, who is a werewolf. So, the concerns of dating someone who is "different" than oneself are represented metaphorically through their relationship. This is also seen in *Sabrina the Teenage Witch*, with Sabrina's relationship with Harvey, who is a mortal, and the prejudice against that in the magical realm. Sabrina and Harvey's relationship will be discussed in more detail later in this chapter, as well as Alex and Mason's.

While the cultural constraints are more symbolic, the qualities of positive, healthy romantic relationships are more explicitly portrayed. Like the portrayal of friendship as discussed in the previous chapter, the modeling of healthy, successful romantic relationships can be studied in these programs. Also connected to the previous chapter on friendship is the emergence of opposite-sex friendships during adolescence and how that contributes to the development of romantic relationships during this age period. One thing that is notably absent in these programs is the portrayal of any same-sex romantic relationships. That discussion is tangled up with issues not only of culture, but also of the business of children's broadcasting, and were not considered for this book. Though not considered, it is worthy of future exploration and research.

The remainder of this chapter will look at various matters related to adolescent romantic lives through a discussion of those characters who: (1) do NOT get involved in major romantic relationships; (2) exhibit romantic feelings for other characters but do not fully act on them; (3) get involved in long-term romantic relationships that do NOT endure; and finally (4) get involved in long-term relationships that ultimately endure. By differentiating it in this way, we can distill various issues related to adolescent romantic lives introduced earlier in this chapter.

Characters that Do Not Get Involved in Romantic Relationships

Not every adolescent gets involved in a romantic relationship, and secret-identity tween sitcoms illustrate this. The main characters that will be used to illustrate this are all three bionic sibling characters of *Lab Rats*, Kaz of *Mighty Med*, Henry Hart of *Henry Danger*, Amy of *Villains of Valley View*, and Violet on *Ultra-Violet & Black Scorpion*.

During the four seasons of *Lab Rats* and one season of *Lab Rats: Elite Force*, none of the bionic siblings, Chase, Adam, or Bree, enter into long-term romantic relationships. There are some episode-specific instances of the characters dating, but nothing serious. The sibling that dates the most is Bree, but there is not much mention of Adam or Chase having much interest in others in a romantic way.

Similarly, on the two seasons of *Mighty Med*, Kaz does not have any long-term romantic interests. In Season 2 Episode 12 "Sparks Fly" he does date a superhero, Sparks, but he finds her too clingy and overly aggressive. He wants to break up with her, but he is literally afraid she will "crush" him if he breaks up with her. So, instead of handling this tough situation, he decides to fake his own death. This of course backfires and he has to break up with her. He admits he was too immature to be dating anyone, "I never should have asked you at all."

On *Henry Danger*, Henry Hart dates a bit, but he doesn't have any long-term love interests. His most important relationships are his friendships with Charlotte and Jasper. In Season 5 Episode 16 "I Dream of Danger" both he and Charlotte have dreams about the other where they kiss, but they do not act on them or even tell the other about them. They know that they are better off as friends, and do not want to risk their friendship. This reflects a typical adolescent happening. Adolescent friend groups are sometimes launching pads for romantic relationships (Connolly et al. 2004).

In *Villains of Valley View*, Amy does not exhibit romantic interest in anyone. It will be interesting to see what will happen with Amy in this area in future seasons. Now that Amy is learning to trust others and make friends, she may evolve into other types of relationships as well.

Similarly, on *Ultra-Violet & Black Scorpion*, Violet does not show any romantic interest in anyone. This could be due to the fact that she is the youngest of our protagonists, at 13 years old. Viewers of the program do get some insight into burgeoning relationships and their issues. Her partner/uncle, Black Scorpion/Cruz, does begin dating Catalina, and seems very happy at first. Then he discovers that she is really Cascada and even though he tries to separate the two, their difference in values cannot be overcome and they break up.

Characters Who Exhibit Romantic Feelings for Others, But Do Not Get Into Relationships

Crushes are a normal part of adolescent romantic development. As such, we do see characters on secret-identity tween sitcoms who have crushes on other characters that do not end up in romantic relationships with them. The exemplary characters for this category are Leo Dooley on *Lab Rats*, Jake and Starling on *Villains of Valley View*, and Skylar and Oliver on *Mighty Med*.

For most of the four seasons of *Lab Rats*, Leo Dooley has a crush on Janelle. There are times when Janelle seems that she may have romantic interest in Leo as well, but the stars never align for them to come together. In Season 1 Episode 11 "Back from the Future" a Leo from a possible future – 7 years from the present – comes back in time. Future Leo and Janelle are a couple. But because Leo intervenes to help his siblings (which his future self-warned him about) he misses the date with Janelle that would have instigated their future relationship. The viewers sees that Future Leo ends up without Janelle. Putting family first is a consistent theme we've seen in past chapters and will see in future chapters as well.

Another couple that looks like they might become romantically involved, but don't, are Jake and Starling on *The Villains of Valley View*. As mentioned in an earlier chapter, Starling is the superhero that saved Jake Madden and inspired him to learn to become good. In Season 1 Episode 6 "Super Secrets" Starling discovers that Jake is really Chaos and wants to turn him (and his family) into the Superhero League. However, once she talks to Hartley about how hard he is trying to be a better person, she decides to keep his secret. We begin to see a little mutual attraction between the two. This becomes more evident in Season 1 Episode 15 "A Superhero in Valley View." Jake convinces Starling to hide out in Valley View after the Superhero League takes away her powers for not turning Chaos in. Jake and Starling's verbal and nonverbal behavior make it clear that they like each other. Hartley and Amy help Starling devise a plan to keep Jake safe and clear Starling's name with the Superhero League, and it works. If they were anyone else but a superhero and an ex-supervillain, they might attempt a romance. But alas, that is impossible … for now.

The last two characters that exhibit feelings for each other but do not act on them are Skylar and Oliver on *Mighty Med*. Even before Oliver discovered Mighty Med he had a crush on superhero Skylar Storm. When he meets her at Mighty Med, he is obviously still interested in her romantically. However, he does not act on his feelings. He befriends Skylar and helps her to adjust to life without her powers. Throughout the two seasons of *Mighty Med*, and on the only season of *Lab Rats: Elite Force*, Oliver continues to have feelings for Skylar. There are times when Skylar hints that she shares those feelings, but she does not act on them. On Season 1 Episode 24 "There's a Storm Coming" (Season finale) she does kiss him on the cheek to thank him for returning her powers. Oliver's gesture backfires on him, however, and while she has her powers back, the process has turned her evil. The second season of the programs centers on Oliver trying to turn Skylar back to good. When that finally happens, Oliver is just happy to have her back, even as friends.

The emphasis of the importance of friendship seen on these last two examples continues the messages described in the previous chapter.

Long-lasting Relationships that Do Not Endure

While many adolescents do get involved in romantic relationships, not all of them will endure into young adulthood and beyond. K.C. and Brett have an ongoing relationship on *K.C. Undercover* that does not stand the test of time. Similarly, in *The Thundermans*, both siblings, Phoebe and Max, have serious relationships that do not last.

In *K.C. Undercover*, we sometimes see K.C.'s spy cover involve her flirting with an antagonist. Sometimes those flirtations go a little further and K.C. has to go on a date with someone involved in her mission. With one of those people, Brett, the line between K.C. the spy and K.C. the regular girl got a little blurred, and she thought she might have feelings for the person. The beginning of K.C. and Brett's relationship is the focus of a three-part story arc "Double-Crossed Parts 1-3 (Season 1, Episodes 10-12)." Brett is also a spy, and K.C. and Brett are ordered by The Organization to pretend to be in a relationship for a mission. K.C. develops real feelings for Brett, but finds out that Brett likes Marissa, so she backs off. Eventually Marissa figures out that K.C. likes her, and tells K.C. she is going to break it off with Brett. K.C. warns Brett that Marissa is going to break up with him and he confesses that he really has feelings for K.C.

K.C. and Brett start dating, but on one date Brett tells K.C. he is taking her to a concert, but in reality he takes her to his father, a criminal named Zane. It turns out that Brett is a double agent. Still, when K.C. asks him if any of his feelings for her were ever real, he admits they were. Eventually K.C. escapes and battles with Brett, and she breaks up with him.

Brett comes into the picture again on Season 1, Episode 17, when K.C. infiltrates The Other Side and Brett is her combat instructor. Brett does not turn K.C. in and when Victor, the leader of the Other Side, tries to destroy K.C., Brett comes in and saves her and helps her escape.

K.C. and Brett's relationship comes full circle during the two-part season finale of Season 1 "K.C. and Brett: The Final Chapter, Parts 1 and 2." Brett is in trouble for not being able to eliminate K.C., but K.C. and her family agree to hide him. This allows K.C. and Brett to spend some time together, and it is obvious they both have feelings for one another. However, in the end, Brett has to escape to Canada, and he and K.C. agree they can never see each other again. While it was clear that they loved each other and that neither could physically hurt the other, their relationship was doomed to fail. This relationship illustrates an exaggerated version of an adolescent romantic relationship that is based on mutual attraction, but not necessarily sustainable due to differing core values.

Differences in values and culture also colored the romantic partnerings of the Thunderman twins, Phoebe and Alison. Phoebe had a long-term relationship with the son of her dad's nemesis, Link Evilman. Given his last name, you might think that Link wanted to follow in his father's footsteps and be a supervillain like his father. But in reality, Link wanted to be a superhero.

Phoebe and Link's relationship initiated due to shared affinity, as many adolescent relationships do. When Phoebe accidentally exposed her superpowers to Link at Splatburger, she goes over to try to cover it up, but he confesses he has superpowers too. They are both excited to not have to hide their powers from someone. But when she figures out who Link is related to, she knows it will cause trouble in the family if she dates him, given their fathers' history. They were right in their concern, as both parents forbade their children from dating. However, Link and Phoebe stick up for themselves with their parents and remind them that they should not have to suffer for their parents' problems. Link and Phoebe's relationship lasts through most of Seasons 2 and 3, and they go through a number of typical "adolescent relationship" problems. In one episode, Phoebe thinks Link is too clingy, while in another she gets jealous that Link is spending too much time with her brother Max, but they do have superhero problems as well. The Hero League asks Phoebe to spy on Link's dad, because they think he is doing something bad. This leads Phoebe to question Link's intentions and erodes their trust a bit. When Phoebe realizes that Link really wants to be a superhero, she helps train him, but she does her job so well that the Hero League recruits him to work for them in Hong Kong, and they mutually decide to break up. But they do remain friends, and he returns to take Phoebe to prom, as a friend.

That prom is the episode discussed in a previous chapter where Max gives up his dreams of being a supervillain and turns superhero. As a reminder, Phoebe convinced Max not to steal her powers by asking him, "Is that really what you want Max? To lose everything? Your friends? Allison? Your family?" When Dark Mayhem asks him, "What are you waiting for, Max. You're this close to having it all!" Max looks around at his friends, his girlfriend, and his family and responds with tears in his eyes, "I already do." Allison is an important part of Max's choice. So how did their relationship begin?

Allison and Max first meet in Season 3 Episode 8 "Floral Support," when Phoebe tries to get Max to join Allison's environmental club. After initially trying to sabotage the club, Max ends up helping them. In Season 3 Episode 12 "Date Expectations" Phoebe lies to both Allison and Max and tells each of them the other wants to go on a date. Phoebe is trying to get Max back for bothering her at home, and she also is trying to distract Allison, who is representing Greenland in their Model U.N. project. Phoebe thinks that Allison's environmental demands are going to impact her grade on the Model U.N. project. While on their fake date, Allison opens up to Max and tells him that her parents don't support her with her environmental causes because they just think she is just going through a phase. This resonates with Max because his parents think he's going through an evil phase as well. This similarity creates an affinity between Max and Allison, and they start to date for real.

On the next episode, Season 3, Episode 13 "He Got Game Night" they officially become boyfriend and girlfriend. They continue as boyfriend and girlfriend for the remainder of Season 3, including the earlier mentioned Season 3 finale when Max decides to be a superhero and the Thundermans' big secret is revealed to all of Hiddenville. Max and Allison are still together at the beginning of Season 4. Allison goes away to volunteer helping the environment for 3 months and just when she is about to return, she texts Max and breaks up with him, telling him that "the earth is my soulmate now." Max is devastated. He spirals into a depression, spending most of his time sleeping and eating pizza with Dr. Colosso, and stops showering. After a couple days, Phoebe goes into Max's Lair and tries to get him back to Z-Force training, but Max is not ready yet. When Phoebe insists on trying to cheer him up, Max tries to freeze her but his freeze-breath is too weak and short to even reach her. The break-up has affected his powers. Phoebe tries to convince Max to get over Allison and move on. She tells him that he shouldn't put his life on hold just because Allison broke up with him. She gives him the

> plenty of fish in the sea" argument, but Max argues that no other girl will ever be like Allison. Allison was his first real girlfriend and she understood him. He doesn't think he will ever be able to love again. However Max is jolted into moving on after hearing Principal Bradford saying that he has never loved again since his ex broke his heart. He realizes that if he doesn't get over Allison, he will end up as miserable as he puts it "Sad Tad Bradford ... and nobody wants that.

So, Max gets the courage to move on. To illustrate the change of heart, we see his powers return as he uses them to save Phoebe from getting caught by Bradford. Max's relationship with Allison illustrates young, first love and heartbreak and how to deal with it.

Long-lasting Relationships that Ultimately Endure

In real life and in "reel life" there are some relationships that stand the test of time. Some stay together from the very beginning, while others break up and find their way back to one another in the long run. The characters used to demonstrate this will be Sabrina and Harvey on *Sabrina the Teenage Witch*; Max and Talia, Justin and Juliet, and Alex and Mason on *Wizards of Waverly Place*; and Miley, Jake, and Jesse on *Hannah Montana*.

On Sabrina Spellman's 16th birthday and first day at her new school, she meets Harvey Kinkle. Over the course of the first four seasons of the program, when Sabrina and Harvey are in high school, they are in a romantic relationship. A number of times during this period, Harvey figures out that Sabrina is a witch. Each time, however, she is able to use her magic to make him forget. During these four years, Harvey has had some competition for Sabrina's heart.

In Season 2, Episode 25 "Rumor Mill" Sabrina meets another half-witch/half-mortal like herself, Dashiell. She meets Dashiell while they are both doing community service in The Other Realm. She starts to see him while still seeing Harvey. She is conflicted. The things she has in common with Dashiell make her think she should be with him, but she still wants to be with Harvey as well. She casts a "Follow Your Heart" spell which causes the two to literally fight for her love. The spell determines that Harvey is the one that she really wants to be with. In addition, as a witch, Dash figures out what spell it was, so he gives up and decides to remain friends with Sabrina.

Harvey's biggest competition during these high school years was Josh. Harvey is jealous of Sabrina's relationship with Josh, who is her boss at the coffee shop she works at. At first Josh and Sabrina are just friends, but in Season 4 Episode 7 "Prelude to a Kiss" Josh and Sabrina kiss, and Harvey witnesses it. Sabrina and Harvey break up. In Season 4 Episode 9 "Love Means Having to Say You're Sorry" Sabrina tries to get Harvey to forgive her. She wants to be with him, not Josh. She overhears Harvey saying that he still loves her but that he doesn't think he could ever forgive her for what she has done. She tries a number of spells to try make Harvey forgive her. None of them work. Eventually she just tells him she's sorry. They start talking again and he eventually forgives her. Sabrina reflects on her apology, "Sometimes the mortal way IS the magic way."

Even though Harvey forgives Sabrina, he is still jealous of Josh and gets upset that Sabrina is still working with him at the coffee shop. Sabrina herself wonders why she isn't willing to stop working with Josh – does she still like him? To find out she enrolls in a magic "boyfriend course" which turns out to be an obstacle course that Josh and Harvey must run through to see who she should choose. It ends in a tie, but more importantly, Sabrina learns that mortals have a quota on how much magic can be used on them, and Harvey has reached his quota. She can no longer use a memory spell on him to make him forget any magic he's encountered. This means he is going to remember the "boyfriend course." In the very last scene, of this last episode of Season 4, Harvey confronts Sabrina, "Can we talk about the fact that you're a witch?"

When this episode originally aired, this was written to be a series finale, and not just a season finale. The show moved to another network the next season and producers totally reworked the show. This included having Sabrina attend college, and it did NOT include Harvey. So, in the season premiere of Season 5, viewers learned that Harvey broke up with Sabrina after learning she was a witch. She ends up dating Josh again in Season 6, but he ends up taking a job in Prague.

During the final season of the show, Sabrina is now a young adult and she meets a nice guy, Aaron, at her new job at a magazine. They begin to date, but Aaron is jealous that Sabrina is still friends with Harvey. During the final season Aaron and Sabrina become engaged and in the series finale, they are set to marry. But Sabrina begins to question whether or not she is her true soulmate. In the end, even without magic, she realizes that her heart is not with Aaron. She calls off the wedding, and when she leaves the church, who is there to ride off into the sunset with her, but Harvey. He is her true soulmate.

Sabrina's journey is unique in the fact that we have 7 seasons to watch Sabrina's choices when it comes to romance. When looking at Sabrina's story as a whole, Harvey was her first love and her last love, and he was always her friend. Their relationship illustrates the importance of trust and loyalty and also the old adage, "If you love something set it free. If it comes back to you it's yours. If it doesn't it was never meant to be." The connection to this saying is not that our destiny is predetermined, but rather that you can't make people love you, and that sometimes the timing just needs to be right.

While it was always fairly obvious who Sabrina's true soulmate was, for Miley Stewart, it wasn't always so clear. Over the course of four seasons, there were two people who stole Miley's heart: Jake and Jesse.

Jake was Miley's first love. Jake Ryan was a famous young actor who started attending Miley's school part time. While the rest of the school was impressed with his celebrity status, Miley was not. Given that she was a secret-celebrity as well, it was easy for Miley to look past all the glitz and glamour that Jake exhibited, which actually intrigued Jake. While everyone else was trying to become friends with Jake, Miley treated him very regularly, to the point of sometimes being rude. Things with Jake get complicated when Jake has to work with Hannah Montana. He ends up talking to Hannah about "this girl at school who he likes, Miley." This makes Miley see him in a different light. She reveals to Jake that Hannah and Miley are the same person and eventually she agrees to go out with him.

Miley gets annoyed by all the paparazzi attention whenever she and Jake go out, so Jake tries to go "incognito" and he doesn't like not having the benefits of celebrity. This turns off Miley. She wants to break up with Jake, but she is afraid he is going to reveal her secret. Jake gets upset that Miley would think he could do that. Here again, the theme of trust in relationships is prevalent. Jake realizes that he really doesn't know how to be a "normal" person anymore, and that until he figures that out, he'll leave Miley alone. In the final season they start to date again, but Jake ends up cheating on her and they break up.

Before Miley and Jake break up, Miley tries to hide their relationship from her dad (who is not a Jake fan) by dating the guitarist from her band, Jesse, in Season 3 Episodes 18 and 19 "He Could Be the One: Parts 1 and 2." Miley starts to develop real feelings for Jesse and has to decide who she wants to be with Jesse or Jake. She ultimately chooses Jake. But when Jake cheats on Miley in the fourth season she breaks up with him and is single again. In Season 4 Episode 6 "Been Here All Along" Miley bumps into

Jesse on the pier. Jesse only knew "Hannah" so it is an awkward exchange. In Season 4, Episode 9

> I'll Always Remember You (Part 1)" Miley decides to tell Jesse the truth about Miley and Hannah. Things are going great until Hannah and Jesse kiss after playing a song on *The Tonight Show*. Then the paparazzi catches Jesse kissing Miley and thinks he's cheating on Hannah. This becomes one of the impetuses for Miley to tell the world she is Hannah Montana in Season 4, Episode 10, "I'll Always Remember You
>
> (Part 2).

As the series ends, Miley and Jesse are still together. But Jesse did not ASK her to tell her secret. He supported her choice either way. He loves both sides of her and lets her make her own decision.

The secret-identity tween show that has the most long-term sustainable romantic relationships is *Wizards of Waverly Place*. At the conclusion of the series, each of the Russo siblings, Max, Justin, and Alex, all have long-term significant others.

Max is the youngest Russo sibling. When *Wizards of Waverly Place* began he was just 12 years old. Over the course of four seasons, he dated a bit, but his only serious girlfriend was Talia. They begin dating in Season 4, Episode 11 "Back to Max." But in episode 13 "Magic Unmasked" Talia starts to ask Max to do things that he really doesn't like. He pretends to like things for her, but he finally tells her that they should break up because he really doesn't like the things she likes. Talia decides to try some things that Max likes and she has fun. She apologizes to Max and they decide that it is okay to like different things. By the end of the series they are still dating, and Max becomes mortal (since he loses the family wizarding contest), so he never has to tell her about being a wizard. Max and Talia's relationship is quantitatively the shortest of the siblings because it starts last, and it is also the least mature, since Talia and Max are about 15 years old.

The oldest Russo sibling, Justin, also has the longest-portrayed romantic pairing on the show. Justin meets Juliet Van Heusen on Season 2, Episode 26 "Wizards vs. Vampires on Waverly Place." Juliet's family opens a restaurant that is competing with the Russo's submarine shop, and Justin goes to investigate. He meets Juliet and there is a definite connection. They start to date. Justin learns that Juliet and her family are vampires, and once they begin seeing each other, Juliet discovers that Justin is a wizard, because she has a powerful sense of smell, and wizards give off a distinct odor. Both Justin's and Juliet's parents do not want them to be together and demand that they break up. They are both heartbroken.

Juliet's parents eventually see how much Justin loves Juliet, so they acquiesce. It takes Justin's parents a little longer. They realize that just because they do not like the Van Heusen's they can't get in the way of Justin's and Juliet's happiness.

For some time Justin happily dates Juliet. He vacations with her family and they go to prom together. But in Season 3 the wizards and vampires get into a battle with other magical creatures. One of those creatures is Juliet's former boyfriend, Mason the werewolf. Mason wants to get Juliet back and while he runs to catch her, he accidentally scratches her. Juliet sadly tells Justin that when a vampire get scratched by a werewolf, they turn their actual age, and she is 2,193 years old. She transforms into an old woman and leaves Justin behind. He is heartbroken and finds it difficult to move on. He does eventually attempt to date again, and we glimpse an "old" Juliet watching him from afar. In the final season, Juliet returns when the angel of darkness, Gorog, makes her young again and puts her in a trance. He uses her to try to recruit Justin to the dark side. Justin and his siblings work together to destroy Gorog and rescue Juliet. Justin and Juliet reunite and remain together for the remainder of the series. At the family wizarding competition, Juliet is there to cheer him on. Justin and Juliet endure a number of obstacles to be together – they come from different worlds, they have evil beings breaking them apart, but their love persists. The lesson from their love story is that love is not always easy and takes work to last.

We were briefly introduced to the final Russo sibling, Alex's love, in our chapter on morality. Her love, Mason, was also just mentioned in Justin and Juliet's story. The werewolf that used to date Juliet is Alex's love, Mason. Of course Alex doesn't know this at first. She meets Mason at an art class and assumes he is mortal. They start to date, and Alex begins to fall for him. She begins to think that Mason is cheating on her when he always leaves at night. She follows him and discovers he is a werewolf. She confesses her secret that she is a wizard. When Alex reveals Mason's secret to her family, Justin is still depressed about losing Juliet when they had first broken up, so Mason offers to track her down, using his sense of smell. This is how Mason reunites with Juliet and realizes that she was his love over 300 years ago. He actually tells Juliet that he still loves her, so Alex is heartbroken. Mason tries to win Alex back. He comes to the sub shop where Alex is working to beg for forgiveness. He explains that werewolves are loyal but also impulsive and that he doesn't really still love Juliet. This leads to the incident that ages Juliet – the werewolf scratch of a wizard. But that is not the only consequence – in the same battle, Juliet bit Mason, and when a vampire bites a werewolf they turn into a wolf forever. He transforms and leaves Alex in shock and pain. Then, on Season 3, Episode 28, Alex discovers that some backwoods wizards are keeping Mason the wolf hostage, after seeing a story of a "dog" painting a girl that looks like Alex. The country wizards transform Mason back to human form as a way of trying to trick the Russo's into giving them their portal. After Alex tricks them back, Mason transforms back into a wolf. The siblings work to recreate the transformation spell and it ALMOST works – now Mason is just a werewolf, not a full wolf. Eventually he does turn back into his human form, but not until after Alex realizes that she would love him no matter what he looked like. They are back together and remain so until the end of the series.

Both Justin's and Juliet's and Alex's and Mason's relationship encompass and issue that adolescent romances could face but in symbolic ways. When Mason first brought Alex to meet his parents, they were unhappy because Mason is a pureblood werewolf and they wanted him to be with a pureblood as well. Justin and Juliet had similar hurdles. When Alex was at a party with Mason when he looked like a werewolf, people were treating them differently. This symbolically reflects issues of racism that could occur in interracial romances, or differences in religious backgrounds. It also highlights the parental pressure that is put on adolescent relationships.

The overall storytelling of adolescent romantic relationships covers a range of representations, from not getting involved with anyone romantically, to dating frequently, to getting your heart broken, and finally to finding your soulmate. While not every possibility of romance was addressed, it is also not a standardized story on every show. Characters with secret identities risk a lot to connect to another person and let them know who they truly are. As all teens do.

References

Bowlby, John. 1958. "The Nature of the Childs Tie to His Mother." *International Journal of Psychoanalysis*, *39*, 350–371.

Collins, W. Andrew, Welsh, Deborah P. and Furman, Wyndol. 2009. "Adolescent Romantic Relationships." *Annual Review of Psychology*, *60*, 631–652.

Connolly, Jennifer, Craig, Wendy., Goldberg, Adele and Pepler, Debra. 2004. "Mixed-Gender Groups, Dating, and Romantic Relationships in Early Adolescence." *Journal of Research on Adolescence*, *14* (2) 185–207.

Dornbusch, Sanford M., Ritter, Phillip L., Leiderman, P. Herbert, Roberts, Donald and Fraleigh, Michael. 1987. The Relationship of Parenting Style to Adolescent School Performance. *Child Development*, 58 (5) 1244–1257.

Erikson, Erik. 1950. *Childhood and Society*. W.W. Norton & Co.

Larson, Reed and Wilson, Suzanne. 2004. "Adolescence Across Place and Time: Globalization and the Changing Pathways to Adulthood." In R.M. Lerner and L. Steinberg (Eds.) *Handbook of Adolescent Psychology*. 299–361. John Wiley and Sons, Inc.

Laursen, Brett and Bukowski, William. 1997. "A Developmental Guide to the Organization of Close Relationships." *International Journal of Behavioral Development, 21* (4) 747–770.

Levine, Laura and Munsch, Joyce. 2011. *Child Development: An Active Learning Approach*. Washington DC: Sage.

8 Siblings

As discussed in the previous two chapters, the interpersonal relationships nurtured during adolescence are critical to the development of your identity, and your AIC. While friendships and romances become more of a focal point during adolescence, the interpersonal relationships within families are still the dominant influence in the lives of tweens and teens. As such, they occupy a significant amount of the storytelling in secret-lives tween sitcoms. Given that, we will dedicate the majority of the remainder of this book exploring the portrayal of family on secret-lives tween sitcoms. Some scholars argue that TV families exercise as much influence on real families as the home environment and parents (Singer, Singer, & Rapaczynski, 1984). Signorielli and Morgan (2001) assert that the "importance of television's messages in shaping people's conceptions about families and family life is not trivial" (p 333). While scholars may argue on just how much influence the portrayal of family has on real-world families, there is little debate that media portrayal is one of the many influences on our expectations of family in our own lives.

The next three chapters will explore the portrayal of family on secret-identity tween sitcoms in three different ways. In this chapter we will explore sibling relationships. Chapter 9 will look at parental relationships, and Chapter 10 will investigate the broader family by looking at both extended family and mentor relationships.

If you have a sibling, it is likely to be the longest-lasting interpersonal relationship of your life. You and your sibling(s) are likely to outlive your parents, and you were connected to them before you met any friends or partners. Besides being among the longest-lasting, the sibling relationship also has important implications for adjustment and well-being from childhood through late adulthood (Whiteman, McHale, & Soli, 2011). Dunn explains that sibling relationships are unique in that they include both reciprocal and hierarchical features (1983). They are reciprocal in that siblings are typically relatively close in age and have many shared interests that facilitate frequent interactions (sharing qualities of friendships). They are hierarchical because older siblings typically hold a more powerful,

DOI: 10.4324/9781003593027-8

dominant role within the relationship; this dominance shares qualities with parental relationships. This overlap with peers and parents and the combination of roles they fulfill is something unique to siblings.

Bank and Kahn (1975) describe the importance of loyalty as the foundation of the sibling relationship and describe four functions which siblings perform for each other. First, *identification* and *differentiation* are processes by which siblings see themselves in each other but also distance themselves. Identification occurs when a sibling experiences situations through the lens of the sibling. The sibling realizes that they have things in common with their sibling. When a sibling wants to distinguish themselves from their sibling, and be seen as unique, that is differentiation. Both identification and differentiation contribute to one's self-identity. Bank and Kahn (1975) describe the second function of sibling relationships as mutual regulation. Siblings provide opportunities to test out parts of themselves with their siblings and in turn they serve as advisors to each other. The sibling relationship provides a safe place for such experimentation. Bank and Kahn (1975) identify the third function as providing direct services to each other, such as introduction into a peer group or the teaching of a specific skill. The final function described is how they work together – or apart with parents. This could be forming a coalition with a sibling to rally against something related to a parent, or threatening to tell on a sibling to their parents as a show of control, or something in between.

Still other theoretical perspectives can help us gain insight into the uniqueness of the sibling relationship. Whiteman, McHale, and Soli (2011) provide a thorough synopsis of these differing perspective, but we provide a brief overview of their review here, just to illustrate the scope of standpoints. The Psychoanalytic-Evolutionary perspective includes theories that explore how early sibling relationships impact adult mental health. This includes Attachment Theory (which was discussed in earlier chapters) but also looks at the reciprocity of sibling relationships, the peer-like nature of them, and how family influences personality and issues of resource scarcity (these can be physical resources like money and food as well as emotional resources like love and support). From the Social Psychological lens, Whiteman, McHale, and Soli (2011) identify three specific theories that explain certain ways sibling relationships influence our identity: Attribution Theory, Social Comparison Theory, and Equity Theory. Attribution Theory looks at how people perceive the causes of their lived experiences (what are they ATTRIBUTED TO?). So, what do we blame our siblings for and/or what do we give them credit for in terms of our identity? Festinger's (1954) Social Comparison Theory posits that in order for individuals to develop their own sense of self, they compare themselves to others. Since we spend such a major part of our lives with siblings, they would be someone we would compare ourselves to. During that comparison, if we notice that our sibling(s) are experiencing something that we feel WE should be, but are not, we might think that something is not "fair." This sense of fairness is what Equity Theory would explain.

Whiteman, McHale, and Soli (2011) also explain that Social Learning can provide another perspective of sibling relationships. Older siblings might be seen as role models, but all siblings can use observational learning to learn something from their siblings. The last perspective is the Family Ecological Systems perspective that looks at families as dynamic organisms that are always changing. As such, these systems (families) are open to a number of external influences that can impact the functioning of the family. On the one hand, those external influences can be created by a sibling, but on the other hand another siblings actions could have serious repercussions to the family as a whole.

Much research on siblings looks at these relationships from one or more of these lenses. No matter the lens, the issues of sibling support and conflict are usually addressed. With that in mind, and given the vital role siblings play in identity development in adolescence, it is both interesting and important to explore how siblings are portrayed in these secret-identity tween sitcoms. Do siblings on these programs support each other? What is the nature of conflict between siblings on these programs? Of all the programs studied, there were only two that did not feature siblings: *Sabrina the Teenage Witch* and *Mighty Med.* The remaining programs will be discussed in the rest of this chapter. We will explore the programs with the least number of siblings first and then progress until we get to the show with the largest number of siblings.

Hannah Montana – Miley and Jackson Stewart

Miley and Jackson Stewart are a typical brother and sister. They bicker and make fun of one another, but their love and support are also evident. The episode where this is made most explicit is in Season 1, Episode 6 "Grandma Don't Let Your Babies Grow Up to Play Favorites." Miley and Jackson's grandmother, Mamaw, comes to visit them. Miley thinks it might be to support her, as she is singing (as Hannah Montana) at a tea for the vising Queen of England. But, it turns out that Mamaw is actually in town to support Jackson at a volleyball tournament. Miley is hurt and jealous, especially when Mamaw tells Jackson, "I've never been prouder of a grandchild in all my life." Mamaw hoped to be able to attend the Hannah Montana event before going to Jackson's, but there was a delay, so she has to leave. Hannah is upset. She confronts her grandmother about always putting Jackson first. She tells her, "It makes me feel invisible." Mamaw apologizes, but then queries, "Maybe that's how your brother feels all the time." It is obvious that this hadn't occurred to Miley. She responds, "Really? He never said anything." Mamaw explains "What's he gonna say, sweetie? Don't be Hannah Montana? He wouldn't be a very good brother if he said that, would he?" Miley feels guilty. She realizes just how much Jackson has sacrificed because she is Hannah Montana. Hannah speeds up her event with the queen because she wants to be there for Jackson. But when she arrives at the tournament, she forgets to take off her Hannah paraphernalia. At first she hides, but when Jackson wins and she cheers for him, the audience recognizes Hannah and everyone gives her all of the attention. Afterwards, she and Jackson have a heart-to-heart. Hannah apologizes, "I'm sorry. I didn't mean to mess this up for you. I think Hannah Montana does that a lot." Jackson tries to make her feel better by answering "It's ok." But Miley continues, "No it's not. I don't blame you if you hate me." Jackson explains, "I don't hate you, Miley. Sure, I'd like a little more attention sometimes. But at the end of the day, I like who I am, and that's all that really counts." They hug and Hannah makes an observation, "I think this is the nicest conversation we've ever had." Jackson concurs, "I know – if you tell anyone about it, I'll deny it."

Jackson and Miley's mutual envy and jealousy in this episode are exaggerated versions of the competition for affection that can take place between siblings. From this early episode throughout Hannah Montana's entire four-season journey, Jackson is consistently in her corner. He never betrays her secret, even when it could help him … or when it gets in the way of his own life. Miley also supports Jackson's endeavor. They both act as confidants, and sometimes even partners-in-crime. They are an exemplary portrayal of loyal, supportive siblings – who also drive each other crazy.

Henry Danger – Henry and Piper Hart

Another brother/sister pairing who have a love-hate relationship is Henry and Piper Hart on *Henry Danger*. One distinction between *Henry Danger* and *Hannah Montana* is that for almost five full seasons, Piper does not know that her brother is Kid Danger. When the show begins, Henry is 13 years old and his younger sister, Piper, is around 9 or 10. She is portrayed as an "annoying little sister" for much of the first three seasons. She doesn't have a noticeably close relationship with her brother. She is used as a complicating factor many times, to make Henry's secret harder to keep. She is portrayed as demanding, temperamental, and self-centered. As the seasons progress, and she matures, those qualities tame down a bit.

Piper discovers that her brother is Kid Danger towards the end of the fifth season of the program, on Season 5, Episode 23 "Sister Twister, Part 1." By coincidence, Piper witnesses Captain Man and Kid Danger emerging from their Man Cave. Piper finds the tube and climbs through it. She ends up in the Man Cave just as Henry is chewing his "superhero" gumball that transforms him into Kid Danger. Piper sees the entire transformation and realizes her brother is Kid Danger. Captain Man/Ray wants to wipe her memory, but she ends up wiping his memory by mistake. After much hullabaloo, his memory is restored, and Piper has finagled her way onto the team. Once Henry and Piper start working together, they still bicker, but they definitely get along much better than before. It is important to note that at this point in Season 5, Piper is now closer to 14, so she is more mature and she and Henry have more things in common. Piper and Henry don't share any emotional revelations with each other, or anything like that after the revelation, but it can be inferred that Piper understands her brother a little more after she realizes his secret works to help him and his team.

Ultra-Violet & Black Scorpion – Violet and Santiago Rodriquez

The last set of two siblings is also another brother and sister: Violet and Santiago Rodriguez. Santiago is Violet's older brother. When we first meet Violet, before the mask presents itself to her and she becomes Ultra-Violet, we get a sense that Violet feels inferior to her brother. Her brother is so good at everything he does that he can't keep track of what he won his latest trophy for. While his parents overly gush about Santiago's accomplishments, he is pretty humble about them and plays them down. Still, Violet feels inferior, which is one reason why she is so excited to be given superpowers. There is no overt conflict between Violet and Santiago. They are very supportive of each other. Santiago becomes a little worried that Violet is hiding something, but Violet does not share her secret with him. At the end of Season 1 (which turned out to be the end of the series as well), Santiago is looking in Violet's closet for a game and finds the mask. The show ends with him asking Violet, "Is this what you've been hiding? Why do you have this? Put it on."

Interestingly, Violet is not the only one who was hiding something from the family. We learn that Santiago has secretly been dreaming of becoming a fashion designer. He especially loves designing costumes and masks for luchadores. Violet finds out and is very supportive. She tries to convince him to tell their parents. We only have one season to learn about Violet and Santiago's relationship, but we do get a sense that they love and support each other.

K.C. Undercover – K.C., Ernie, and Judy Cooper

Different family dynamics occur when there are more than two siblings. This is evident on *K.C. Undercover*, as we start off with a sibling dyad of K.C. and her younger brother Ernie. They are later joined by a robot "sibling" Judy. At first, K.C. and Ernie have dynamic that is similar to Violet and Santiago. K.C. is portrayed as being good at everything, and Ernie is shown as being more of an afterthought to his family. Ernie is obviously envious of K.C. While the first episode of the program focuses on K.C. being recruited to be a spy, the second episode has K.C. trying to convince her parents, and the Organization, to recruit Ernie as well. She doesn't like lying to him. She explains that they be better spies as a family, since the typical American family has 2 kids. The Organization agrees with that logic, and allows the Coopers to tell Ernie they are spies, but instead of him being the other "kid" the Coopers bring home J.U.D.Y. (Junior Undercover Digital Youth). So now, technically there are 3 Cooper siblings. K.C. still won't give up on having Ernie join the team. She intercepts a mission and has Ernie do it with her to prove he can handle it. Ernie is still not traditional spy material, but his computer skills and performance on the mission convince the Organization to let him be part of the team.

For the remainder of the series, K.C. and Ernie continue to exhibit a close relationship. They do mock and joke around with each other, but they always have each other's backs on missions and at home. Ernie occasionally exhibits his sense of inferiority to K.C., but for the most part he seems happy to be part of the family/team.

Since Judy is a robot, she doesn't technically have emotions, but she still shares interactions with her "siblings." Ernie and K.C. accept her immediately into the family and treat her as family more than a robot. Symbolically, this could be viewed from the lens of an adopted child being brought into a family with biological siblings, but that would require more in-depth research.

The Villains of Valley View – Jake, Amy, and Colby Madden

One family that begins their series with three children are the Maddens. Similar to Judy Cooper, the Maddens do not exhibit much emotion – at first … at least positive emotion. The Maddens are former supervillains who are in hiding in Hiddenville. We learn that youngest sibling, Colby, did not even have a name when he was living in Metropolis, because his power had not emerged yet. When they lived in Metropolis, they were Chaos, Havoc, and Number 3. Colby's power of shapeshifting emerges and his family dubs him "Flashform."

He gets this new moniker during Season 1, Episode 3 "The Villain Experience." Jake and Amy feel bad that Colby never got to experience being a villain with the family. They try to create an experience to have him feel what it was like to be a supervillain, but it backfires. So, to make sure he knows he is part of the family they all put on their supervillain costumes and present him with his own costume and his new supervillain name.

Colby ends up being the most powerful of all the supervillains. In Season 1, Episode 12 "Showdown at the Round" Colby discovers he has additional powers. Vic tells him that it means he is a once-in-a-lifetime supervillain, The Chosen One.

Older siblings Jake and Amy have a supportive relationship. As supervillains they fought superheroes together. As they live in hiding in Valley View, Jake worries that his relationship with his sister Amy is at risk, after Amy discovers his friendship with superhero Starling. Jake tries acting bad again to win back Amy's trust. Amy is happy that her old "Jake" is back, but eventually she realizes that she doesn't want him to change who he is just for her. Hartley explains to them "You [Jake] shouldn't have to change who you are just to have her forgive you; and if you [Amy] are only forgiving someone because of what they're doing for you, that's not really forgiveness."

Later in the season Amy and Jake band together to save Colby from the head of all supervillains, Onyx. They have to return to Metropolis to rescue him, but it is almost too late. Since Colby is the chosen one, Onyx kidnaps him and uses mind control to make him bad. Colby attempts to destroy his family. Amy tries to connect to break the spell that is controlling Colby. She pleads with him, "You don't want to hurt us, we're your family." Mom Eva tries as well, "Come on Colby – we love you." The spell is broken and Colby joins his family to fight Onyx. Onyx shames them, "You pathetic creatures. You had so much potential as villains and you threw it all away – for what?" Amy reminds him why they went into hiding to begin with, "To defend our mother." Jake adds, "To show you that the guy with all the power doesn't always win." Onyx immobilizes all of them, but Colby tries to use his special power to fight the immobilization and battle Onyx. Onyx laughs at him, "You're wasting your time. Even as the chosen one you'll never be as powerful as me." Amy yells back, "Maybe not, but you don't stand a chance against the two of us together." Amy's body is immobilized, but she has sonic power and uses her voice to amplify Colby's powers and they destroy Onyx.

This illustrates a theme that will come up in other shows as well – that we are more powerful together as a family than we are alone.

Wizards of Waverly Place – Justin, Alex, and Max Russo

This theme is also present throughout the four seasons of *Wizards of Waverly Place*. There are a few times when the three wizard siblings, Justin, Alex, and Max, combine their magical powers to have a greater effect. An exemplary episode is Season 4, Episode 10 "Wizards vs. Angels – Part 2" when Justin, Alex, and Max combine their powers to vaporize the leader of the Angels of Darkness, Gorog, when he threatened to invade the Wizarding World.

This is just one of many examples of the three Russo siblings working together. Still, the core story of *Wizards of Waverly Place* is that only one Russo sibling can ultimately be the family wizard. This is made clear from the first episode, and is continually evident throughout all seasons until Season 4, Episodes 28 and 29 "Who Will Be the Family Wizard?" when they compete for the title. The competition involves a number of rounds, but the last round is a massive labyrinth, and whomever emerges from it first wins the title. Justin makes it out first and is declared the Family Wizard. However, he decides he cannot accept this because Alex was about to get out first: Justin had gotten stuck on a tree root and Alex, near the exit, came back to help. So, Justin gives Alex the position of the Family Wizard. Their wizard teacher, Professor Crumbs, is proud of Justin's decision and his high intelligence, and he declares that he is going to retire as Headmaster of Wiz-Tech. He makes Justin the new Headmaster, granting him full wizard powers. So, Alex is the family wizard, Justin is the Headmaster of Wiz-Tech, and Max is set to inherit the sub shop as a mortal. Max always enjoyed working at the sub shop and is not terribly disappointed in the final outcome. Alex points out that all three siblings are finally happy at the same time.

The results of the Family Wizarding competition are important because they speak to character growth, especially for Alex. Alex had been consistently portrayed as selfish, so the fact that she was willing to give up being the family wizard to save Justin is very telling. The same goes for Justin, who was always portrayed as very ambitious. He could have taken the title, but he knew Alex deserved it.

This realization of the importance of family was actually the theme of a special *Wizards of Waverly Place* movie that was broadcast on Disney Channel on August 29, 2009. In the film, Alex is mad that her mother won't let her go out, so she casts a spell wishing her parents had never met. This has a number of obvious repercussions. The movie plot focuses on Alex trying to undo the spell. Max has been swept into a vortex. Justin technically still exists, but he has no memory of Alex. Justin loses his memory and Alex becomes emotional and explains who she is – his little sister. She explains that even though they pick on each other, she looks up to him and envious of him. She begs Justin to not leave her alone. Justin tells her that he'd never leave her and that even though he doesn't know her, he believes her, and wants to help. Unfortunately he ends up being sucked into the same vortex that Max was. Desperate, Alex tries to cast a reversal spell. She gives up the powers she earned in this alternate universe to turn things back to the way they were. Time rewinds to right before Alex did the original spell. She takes her punishment from her mother and is appreciative of her mom, her dad, and her brothers. The brothers remember the alternate universe as well, and the entire family gets closer.

Lab Rats and *Lab Rats: Elite Force* – Leo Dooley and Chase, Bree, and Adam Davenport

The Dooley/Davenport family is unique. Chase, Bree, and Adam are bionic siblings. Chase was created by Douglas Davenport using his DNA and that of an unidentified donor. He later created bionic daughter, Bree, using just his own DNA. He had improved his bioengineering and found that a female would be more stable due to the XX chromosome. He later perfected his bioengineering and created sons Chase and Adam. When Douglas' brother and business partner, Donald, found out that he was using the bionic children to do nefarious things, he had them taken away from him and raised them as his own. Years later Donald married Tasha Dooley, who had a son Leo. Leo and Tasha moved in with Donald, but were unaware of the bionic siblings. Leo discovered them and bonded with them, and he and Tasha convinced Donald that they needed to experience life as teenagers, even if they were bionically super-engineered.

So, technically, Leo is Adam, Bree, and Chase's step-brother. He teaches them about life as a typical teen, and they become close friends. As the show progresses, Leo becomes involved in missions with his step-siblings, and even gets a bionic arm, when his arm is injured.

While Adam, Bree, and Chase are technically siblings, they interact more as teammates. There is not much emotion and affection shared between them. Going back to Attachment Theory, it could be argued this is because of the lack of bonding they had with a primary caregiver in their younger life. Still, as they bond with Tasha and Leo, and ultimately both Donald and Douglas, they do become more "human," if not very sibling-like.

The Thundermans – Max, Phoebe, Billy, Nora, and Chloe Thunderman

In contrast to the Davenport bionic siblings, our final set of siblings, The Thundermans, exhibit typical sibling behavior. Siblings Phoebe, Max, Billy, and Nora Thunderman move with their parents to Hiddenville, so that they can lead a "normal" life. Of course, as superheroes, their lives are anything but normal, no matter where they live. Even though they've moved, they still retain their superpowers, and they need to keep them hidden from the citizens of Hiddenville. Phoebe and Max's relationship was discussed in both the chapters on Power and Morality, with Max originally wanting to be a supervillain to differentiate himself from his twin, Phoebe. They do interact regularly with their younger siblings, Billy and Nora, sometimes modeling behavior for them.

It is when their last sibling, Chloe, is born that we see more nurturing familial tendencies in the older siblings, Phoebe specifically. Phoebe is very protective of Chloe when she is first born (she ages to a toddler very fast since she is a superhero). In the same episode that Chloe is born, original youngest sibling, Nora fears that she is going to be displaced now that she is no longer "the baby." She learns that each of them have a place in the family and that the love just multiplies the more people are in the family.

The best example of the sibling relationship on *The Thundermans* comes in the final season, Season 4. This is after Max has decided to become a superhero rather than a supervillain, and he and Phoebe end up training together to vie for a spot on the Z-force. They are chosen to compete as a team, but once the Z-force learns that they don't have a special "twin" power, they separate them and force them to fight each other for the position. It is evident that this is uncomfortable for both siblings, after all they've been through. Max ends up winning and joining the Z-force. But, when his family is in danger and he asks the Z-force to help, the Z-force will not abandon another mission to assist. So, Max gives up the Z-force and tries to rescue his family. Phoebe asks him why he would give up finally being "the best" and he replies, "I realized I couldn't put anything before family." It looks hopeless for the Thundermans. They are locked up with their powers neutralized and about to be destroyed. They all hold hands and when Phoebe and Max join hands, something sparks. It is their twin power! Phoebe suggests, "We had twin power all along. Seeing your family in danger must have activated it." Max counters, "No, pretty sure we never held hands before." Now that their twin power has saved them and neither of them are on the Z-force, they decide to fight crime together, as a team. They add three more members to their team when President Kickbutt tells them that she has removed the old Z-force and wants Phoebe and Max to assemble a new one. They know who they want on their team – the rest of their family. Phoebe summarizes "You guys gave up being superheroes so we could have a normal life. But maybe being a family of superheroes is our normal life."

The Thundermans, Russos, and Maddens all learned that their powers were more formidable when they worked together as a family. All these sibling examples had a mix of conflict and support, as most siblings do. Siblings might bicker, and make fun of each other on these shows, and sibling rivalry is a key storytelling element on a number of these programs. Still, secret-identity tween show siblings always stand by one other and are there whenever their siblings need them.

References

Bank, Stephen and Kahn, Michael. 1975. "Sisterhood-Brotherhood is Powerful: Sibling Sub-Systems and Gamily Therapy." *Family Process, 14* (3) 311–337.

Dunn, Judy. 1983. "Sibling Relationships in Early Childhood." *Child Development*, *54* (4) 787–811.

Festinger, Leon. 1954. "The Theory of Social Comparison Processes." *Human Relations*, *7*, 117–140.

Signorielli, Nancy and Morgan, 2001. "Television and the Family: The Cultural Perspective" in Jennings Bryant and Allison Bryant (Eds.) *Television and the American Family, 2nd edition*. San Francisco Book Company.

Singer, Jerome L., Singer, Dorothy G., and Rapaczynski, Wanda S. 1984. "Family Patterns and Television Viewing as Predictors of Children's Beliefs and Aggression." *Journal of Communication*, *34* (2) 73–89.

Whiteman, Shawn D., McHale, Susan, and Soli, Anna. 2011. "Theoretical Perspectives on Sibling Relationships." *Journal of Family Theory*, *3* (2) 124–139.

9 Parents

In the examples presented in the previous chapter on siblings, the lesson that characters ultimately learned was that they were stronger as a family. While siblings contribute to our sense of self and our identity journey, as do previously discussed friendships and romantic partners, the figures who are typically credited with the most influence in our lives are our primary caregivers.

Before we explore how primary caregivers are portrayed on secret-identity tween sitcoms, let's review some of the theoretical perspectives of adolescence to be reminded of the important role primary caregivers play in our lives.

In Chapter 4, we looked at the various types of power: reward power, coercive power, legitimate power, expert power, and referent power (Giddens 1984). Parents can wield most if not all of these types of power with adolescents. They have the ability to punish and to reward, and they hold a legitimate position of power by being the parent. For secret-identity tween sitcoms, many of the parents also enjoy expert power, through being pop stars, spies, witches, wizards, and superheroes. Referent power is based on established relationships, but it is not guaranteed. If characters do not feel a certain bond with their parent, this type of power might not be applicable.

In Chapter 5, we explored Kohlberg's Stages of Moral Reasoning (1981), with tweens moving from the pre-conventional stage into the conventional stage. In the pre-conventional stage children were being "good" at first because their parents told them to (pre-conventional), and then because they value their various interpersonal relationships (conventional), which still include their parents. Also discussed in Chapter 5 was the Dialectic of Autonomy and Attachment. Relational Dialectic Theory (Baxter and Braithwaite 2008) explains these competing needs to have our own identity and be connected to others, including our parents. According to Relational Dialectics, this dialectic is always present in our interpersonal relationships. Still, the specific context with our parents is most prevalent in adolescence.

DOI: 10.4324/9781003593027-9

In Chapter 6 we reviewed Erikson's Stages of Psychosocial Development (1950), with particular focus on Stages IV and V. Erikson emphasized the critical importance of primary caregivers in the earlier stages of childhood development. Parents still play a significant role in these later stages as well. They are not replaced by peer friendship and romantic relationships. Rather, they continue to influence as we move through the crises of industry and inferiority to develop competency. Their importance persists as we move through the crisis of ego-identity and role-confusion to develop fidelity.

Bowlby's Attachment Theory was introduced in Chapter 7 (1958). According to Bowlby, bonding with other humans is an intrinsic human need, and allows us to learn to regulate our emotions, which helps us live longer, healthier lives. Bonding also teaches us to adapt, which encourages both physical and emotional growth. In other words, we need to interact with others to live better lives.

All of these theories support the notion that our primary caregivers, our parents, are fundamentally important to our journey through adolescence and beyond. They play a critical role in developing our self-identity. In addition to the theories already discussed, Baumrind (1991) offers insight with her explanation of various Parenting Styles. Baumrind originally proposed four parenting styles that combined two important and telling dimensions of parenting: demandingness and responsiveness. She describes demandingness as the extent to which parents control their child's behavior or demand their maturity. Responsiveness refers to the degree to which parents are accepting and sensitive to their children's emotional and developmental needs. By rating the degree of these two dimensions as high or low, she created her original four parenting styles. *Authoritative* parents are rated high for both demandingness and responsiveness. In other words, an authoritative parent exacts some control over their children and expects much, but they are also understanding of their children's needs and emotions. By contrast, a *Permissive* parent is rated low for both demandingness and high for responsiveness. They are not controlling and don't have high expectations of their children, but they are attentive to their needs. When a parent has low demandingness AND low responsiveness, Baumrind identifies them as a *Neglectful* parent. They don't have expectations and they don't attend to their children's needs. If a parent doesn't attend to their children's emotional needs (low responsiveness) but has high expectations of behavior and is controlling, they would be considered *Authoritarian* parents.

Later Baumrind (1991) updated these dimensions and styles. She split the concept of responsiveness into both parental warmth and democratic communication. She also split demandingness into maturity demands and parental control. With these four dimensions, she updated her list of parenting styles to include: *authoritative*, *democratic*, *nondirective*, *authoritarian-directive*, *nonauthoritarian-directive*, *unengaged*, and *good enough*. Most of these are self-explanatory given the dimensions, but let's clarify the distinction between authoritarian-directive and non-authoritarian directive. A directive parent is prescriptive; they tell their children exactly what to do, as opposed to a non-directive parent who gives children space to make their own choices, or a democratic parent who works with their child to help them make a decision. So, a nonauthoritarian-directive parent has more responsiveness, specifically parental warmth, but they still are prescriptive in their demands. An authoritarian-directive parent would be considered highly intrusive. They are prescriptive in their demands, and they exhibit high levels of control and low levels of parental warmth.

Baumrind's parenting styles provide a structure to analyze parenting, but it is important to remember that these styles can vary over time and even with specific children. They are not necessarily easy to test in the real world, but they can guide us in our analysis of parents in the "reel" world of secret-identity tween sitcoms. We will discuss the primary caregiver/parental figure for each program, starting with those parents who are characterized as least attentive and move through to the parents who were properly attentive and finally examine one parent who could be considered overly attentive.

The first parents we will discuss are Vic and Eva Madden from *The Villains of Valley View*. When we first meet Vic and Eva they would definitely be categorized in Baumrind's parenting styles as *Good Enough*. As supervillains, they've instilled mostly negative values into their children. In addition, they were not originally seen as supportive. For example, in Season 1, Episode 2 "Trust No One" Vic and Eva's son is convincing them to stay in Valley View. He tells that he is the first person to ever be nominated for "Student of the Month" after being in school less than a month. Eva responds, "Ah, Jakey, I don't know how you do it, but you always find a way to disappoint us." In another example, in Season 1, Episode 3 "The Villain Experience," Hartley asks Vic and Eva where Colby was whenever they were doing their supervillainy back in Metropolis. Vic confesses, "Ok fine, we left him home to play with the rats." Then, when Colby laments that "I've waited my whole life to get a power to prove that I'm not the runt of the family, and now I'll never get a chance to fight with the rest of you." For one second, we think that Vic might be supportive. He pats Colby and says, "Yeah that's rough." But in the next breath he asks everyone else, "Who wants to do a puzzle?"

As the first season progresses, we start to see Vic and Eva display more "typical" parenting behavior. They begin to use their powers for positive things. Vic creates a special serum that will get him a job, and during the Battle of the Bands, Eva uses her electricity to create a light show onstage for Amy and Hartley. When Eva and Hartley win the Battle of the Bands,

Eva is genuinely happy and proud of them. As she puts it, "I'm really getting this ordinary mom thing down."

As the first season concludes we see that Vic and Eva have come full circle. When Onyx threatens to take Colby, Eva pleads, "Onyx please. Leave him alone. Take me instead." Onyx does take Colby and the rest of the family goes to Metropolis to rescue him. Once they do, Eva asks them, "Is it strange that I kind of miss Texas?" Vic answers, "Not at all. Come on, let's go home."

Another set of parents who could not be categorized as truly supportive would be Jake and Kris Hart on *Henry Danger*. While the Harts aren't neglectful, they are a bit clueless. For five seasons they have absolutely no idea that their son is a superhero. They don't seem to realize that he is gone from the house for long stretches of time. In the final season, we learn that Henry is not graduating from high school because he has missed so much school fighting with Captain Man. This seems to go totally unnoticed by Kris and Jake, until it is too late. Towards the end of the series, in Season 5, Episode 37 "Captain Drex," when Henry does finally reveal himself to his parents to save them, it takes some time and convincing for them to believe it. Jake thinks that Henry hired actors to trick them into thinking he's Kid Danger to get out of trouble for not graduating. Once he chews his gum and transforms into Kid Danger, his parents are finally convinced and when Henry apologizes to them for lying all of these years they respond by saying, "We are so proud of you!" While they are still mad that he isn't graduating they both tell him how much they love him.

The last parental figure that is not traditionally supportive would be Donald Davenport of *Lab Rats*. Unlike Adam, Bree, and Chase's biological father (and Donald's brother) Douglas, Donald is not using the bionics for nefarious purposes. Still, he has kept them hidden and has not provided them with a normal life. It is not until he marries Tasha and she and her son Leo come to live with them that he realizes he needs to give the bionics a better life. Even as he does this, he still interacts with Adam, Bree, and Chase more like an employer than a father. Step-mom Tasha brings warmth into the house and this somewhat rubs off on Donald. Even as Lab Rats spun off in to *Lab Rats: Elite Force*, Donald still seemed more like a team leader than a dad. Baumrind would not likely classify him as an unengaged or good enough parent. He is closer to a nonauthoritarian-directive parent. He displays a certain degree of parental warmth, but he is still prescriptive in his direction. As a team leader he tells them what to do on a mission, and they are expected to follow.

The majority of the parents/primary caregivers on secret-identity tween sitcoms are typically and appropriately attentive. Interestingly, of all of these, only one set of parents is not aware of their child's secret identity. While this is just a correlation, the relationship between being yourself with your family is still important to mention. The parents that do not know but are still supportive are Nina and Juan Carlos Rodriguez on *Ultra-Violet & Black Scorpion*. Since Violet has her Uncle Cruz to serve as mentor (which is discussed in the next chapter), she still has some level of familial support. Before Violet gets her superpower, her parents are supportive of her, even if Violet feels second best to her brother. Her parents do overly praise her brother for all of his accomplishments, but they try to build Violet up as well. Interestingly it is her brother who they ultimately offend when they don't support his dreams of becoming a fashion designer. Still, they do follow Baumrind's democratic parenting style and eventually allow him to make his own decision. The familial warmth of the Rodriguez's is very evident. Mom, Dad, Santiago, and Violet all support one another and show one another affection on a regular basis. It is important to remember that Violet is just 13. Her mother gets very nervous when she goes on her first sleepover in Season 1, Episode 4, "Sleepover Showdown" and gets upset that Violet is sharing her problems with Maya and with her Uncle Cruz instead of her. So, even though her parents don't know her secret, they are concerned she is hiding something and are worried about her safety. Unlike Henry's parents in *Henry Danger*, they are aware of her changes in behavior and are trying to still be supportive.

The remainder of the "typically attentive" primary caregivers/parents all know about their children's secret identity from the beginning. In *Sabrina the Teenage Witch*, Sabrina lives with her aunts, Hilda and Zelda, and they help her navigate her new life as a witch. In *K.C. Undercover*, K.C.'s parents recruit her to join them as spies. Miley Stewart's dad, Robby Ray, helps Miley juggle life as *Hannah Montana*, serving as her manager and regularly donning a mustache to hide his own identity. The Russo siblings of *Wizards of Waverly Place* originally learn magic from their father, Jerry, before also attending Wiz-Tech. And Hank and Barb Thunderman of *The Thundermans* moved their superhero family to Hiddenville to try to give them a normal life. Besides knowing their children's secrets, there are a number of other similarities in the portrayals of these characters. All of them are considered a little "dorky" and embarrassing at times by their children. They all discipline their children when they do something wrong. They all display parental warmth and affection to their children on a regular basis, and would be considered democratic in their communication and decision making.

The differences in these caregivers are more structural than substantive. Hilda and Zelda Spellman are Sabrina's aunts and guardians. Kira and Craig Cooper are married and work together, as do Hank and Barb Thunderman. Robby Ray Stewart is a single widower. Jerry Russo is a former wizard who is married to mortal. Nina and Juan Carlos both work outside the home.

In these typically attentive parented families, there are still conflicts between parents and children, but they are generally resolved in a democratic way. There are some larger scale, longer-term conflicts that deserve some mention. One of these conflicts was already discussed in detail in Chapter 5's discussion of morality: the relationship between Alex Russo and her parents, and how they consistently asked her to "grow up" and change her core nature. In the end they did finally accept her for who she was. Also mentioned in that chapter was Max's struggle to choose between being a superhero and supervillain on *The Thundermans*. When he was about to choose evil, his parents told him that if he went on that path he would no longer be their son. Still, they had supported him up until that point, and even after he stole their powers, they forgave him.

The last parent to discuss is one whose behavior would be hard to forgive. Oliver's mother, Bridget, on *Mighty Med* exemplifies Baumrind's authoritarian-directive parenting style. She is demanding, intrusive, and overbearing. In the first season of *Mighty Med*, we hear more about Bridget by reputation. Her overprotectiveness is apparent in how Oliver has to check in with her and the limitations she puts on his behavior. She does not like Kaz and refers to him as "That One." She takes things to a whole other level during the second season, when it turns out that Bridget is actually Mr. Terror, the criminal mastermind supervillain.

Of course, we don't realize that until it is much too late. At first, we hear about Mr. Terror and his plans to capture comic book writer Quimby Fletcher, who wrote about a powerful space rock, the Arcturion. Viewers know that Quimby Fletcher is a pseudonym for Oliver. Oliver had a dream about the Arcuturion. At the same time, we also learn that Bridget has been dating Dr. Horace Diaz, Oliver's mentor. There are many more details, but the summary is that Bridget has been Mr. Terror all along and was using Horace because she knew that he had the ability to bring one person back to life with his powers, and she wanted it to be her. She knew that if she got the Arcturion and touched it, she would die. If Horace brought her back to life, she would retain her power forever.

Her original motivation for all of her supervillainy behaviors was to try to make the world safe for Oliver, by controlling everything. This extreme take on being a controlling mother backfired, as she became hungry for more power and ended up hurting Oliver, since he was Quimby Fletcher.

At the wedding, everything she hoped for came to pass, as she got the Arcturo and unlimited power. Horace did use his power to bring her back after the Arcturion killed her.

Before the wedding though, Oliver discovers his mother is Mr. Terror and works to defeat her. In the series finale, "The Mother of All Villains, Part 2," Oliver tries to stop her, but she tells him "I told you Oliver, I'm doing this all for you." She escapes, but in the process of the battle, Kaz and Oliver absorb some of Mr. Terror's powers and now have superpowers. Since *Mighty Med* was canceled after this, we don't know what happened to his mother. But later, when *Lab Rats: Elite Force* premieres, it is revealed that Kaz, Oliver, and Skylar eventually defeated and captured her.

Baumrind does not have a parenting style for criminal masterminds, but Bridget symbolically illustrates the most controlling parenting style, authoritarian-directive. She amplifies adolescent concerns of an overprotective, controlling, and intrusive parent. They don't want a supervillain parent who tries to mastermind their lives; they'd prefer a supportive parent who helps them figure out their own path.

References

Baumrind, Diana. 1991. "The Influence of Parenting Style on Adolescent Competence and Substance Use." *Journal of Early Adolescence, 11* 56–95.

Baxter, Leslie A. and Braithwaite, Dawn O. 2008. "Relational Dialectics Theory." In Leslie A. Baxter and Dawn O. Braithewaite (Eds). *Engaging Theories in interpersonal Communication: Multiple Perspectives*, 349–361. Sage Publications.

Bowlby, John. 1958. "The Nature of the Childs Tie to His Mother." *International Journal of Psychoanalysis*, *39*, 350–371.

Erikson, Erik. 1950. *Childhood and Society*. W.W. Norton & Co.

Giddens, Anthony. 1984. *The Constitution of Society. Outline of the Theory of Structuration*. University of California Press, Berkeley.

Kohlberg, Lawrence. 1981. *The Philosophy of Moral Development: Moral Stages and the Idea of Justice*. San Francisco: Harper & Row.

10 Extended Family and Mentors

Siblings and parents are not the only family in adolescents' lives. Extended family could play an influential role in the lives of young people as well. However, there were limited representations of extended family on secret-lives tween sitcoms. The few depictions that were observed will be reviewed in the following paragraphs. After that, a brief discussion on the role of mentorship on these programs will also be included. While not strictly related to family, there was a pattern of portrayal of the importance of mentorship that deserves mention.

Research has shown that extended family members, especially grandparents, can assist in passing on cultural teachings and traditions, including language. The connection with extended family is also connected to the children's healthy self-esteem (Scales and Giboons, 1996). Given the importance that extended family can have in the lives of young people, it is surprising that there was not more attention to this dynamic found in secret-lives tween sitcoms.

In fact, the only mention of aunts and cousins found in these programs was on *K.C. Undercover*, and the relationship was adversarial. Kira Cooper, K.C.'s mother, had a sister, Erica King, who worked for The Other Side with her husband, Richard and her daughter Abby. Erica harbored jealousy for her sister and their parents and it manifest in her becoming a criminal. The majority of Season 2 involves the battle between the Coopers and Erica and her family. There is no love lost between Kira and her sister, and in turn their daughters, cousins K.C. and Abby. Kira and Erica's tale is a cautionary sibling story of jealousy going too far and driving behavior in a negative way.

Before we ever met Erica, we learned that Kira and Erica's parents (K.C.'s grandparents) were also spies. In Season 1, Episode 4, "Off The Grid" K.C. and Ernie team up with Grandma and Pops to rescue their parents from a dangerous mission. Pops never shows up again, and we see Grandma just one more time in Season 3, Episode 17 "Take Me Out." Craig's father (who is NOT a spy) comes to visit during Season 3, Episode 16 "The Gammy Files."

DOI: 10.4324/9781003593027-10

Another show that features grandparents who are in the "family business" is *The Thundermans*. We only meet Nana and Pop-Pop Thunderman in one episode, and it is close to the end of the series. In Season 4, Episode 24 "Make It Pop Pop" Nana and Pop-Pop come to visit. Phoebe becomes jealous when Pop-Pop only wants to spend time with Max. Pop-Pop overhears Phoebe telling Max that their grandfather would not be so proud of him if he knew that Max was keeping Dr. Colosso (Max's pet rabbit/evil mentor) in his villain lair. Pop-Pop transforms into his superhero alter-ego "Sergeant Thunder" and flies to get a device to send Dr. Colloso to the Detention Zone. The Detention Zone is a dimension where supervillains are sent to suffer. When Max tries to convince Pop-Pop not to send Dr. Colosso to the Detention Zone by explaining that he is his friend, Pop-Pop decides to send Max there too. Phoebe ends up using her powers to freeze Pop-Pop and rescue Max and Dr. Colosso. In the end we learn that Pop-Pop was giving Max more attention than Phoebe because he had just recently turned good and he didn't want him to go back to being evil. Pop-Pop's view of the world as being strictly good vs. evil could be viewed as a generational difference of values. It also illustrates the influence that grandparents and other extended family members can have on a young person's value formation.

As mentioned in the chapter on sibling relationships, Miley and Jackson Stewart's grandmother, Mamaw, also plays a minor role in *Hannah Montana*. In Season 1, Episode 6 "Grandma Don't Let Your Babies Grow Up to Play Favorites" Mamaw showed how she wanted to make sure the Jackson didn't feel overshadowed by Miley/Hannah. Mamaw visits in other episodes throughout the series and is portrayed as having a hard time accepting that Jackson and Miley are growing up. Towards the end of the series, after Miley reveals that she is Hannah Montana, Mamaw and Miley have some conflict when Miley's fans keep her from enjoying time with her granddaughter. In Season 4, Episode 12 "I am Mamaw, Hear Me Roar" Mamaw becomes angry when she can't even get a graduation picture with Miley. Miley assures Mamaw that while their private time will need to be a little more private now, it will always mean as much to her as it does to Mamaw. This was the most extended and consistent portrayal of the importance of grandparents in the lives of adolescences seen in secret-identity tween sitcoms.

In addition to these portrayals of extended family, we do learn a bit about the extended Russo family on *Wizards of Waverly* place in flashbacks of how the dad, Jerry, gave up his wizarding powers to his brother. Like Justin, Alex, and Max, Jerry had to compete to become family wizard with his siblings, brother Kelbo and sister Megan. Jerry won the family competition but gave up being a wizard to marry Therese. He gave his power to Kelbo. His sister Megan was mad that he did this, but Jerry explained that he only did it because he knew that Megan would be fine without powers, but Kelbo would not. In addition to Kelbo and Megan, in the final episode of *Wizards of Waverly Place* we glimpse some of the extended Russo family at a family reunion in Italy, but it is extremely limited.

The one show where an extended family member plays a major role is *Ultra-Violet & Black Scorpion*. Violet's uncle, Cruz, is also Ultra-Violet's superhero partner, Black Scorpion. In Season 1, Episode 1 "The Violet behind the Ultra" we meet Cruz and see that he does not have a very close relationship with his sister and her family, no matter how many times Violet tries to include him in family dinners. However, over the course of the season, as Black Scorpion works closely with Ultra-Violet, Violet and Cruz get closer in turn. They support each other. When Violet's friend Maya was mad at her, Cruz was there as a shoulder to cry on. Similarly, Violet encouraged Cruz at all stages of his romantic relationship with Catalina. During the series finale, Cruz praises Violet, "Tonight, you were the real hero." She responds, "It's only because you taught me so much." While Black Scorpion was teaching Ultra-Violet to be a superhero, Violet was showing Cruz how to be a better uncle and brother. After working with Violet, he realized that since he became a superhero, he had been shutting himself off to people, especially his family. The series began with Cruz missing a family dinner and it concluded with Cruz bringing dinner to his family and enjoying their company. He even offers a toast, "Salud. Amor. Mi familia." Health. Love. My family.

Cruz is an excellent example of the important role nonparental adults can fill in the lives of young people. Nonparental adults can be a source of social support. In addition they can play a part in a young person's educational achievement and personal development. They allow adolescents to try new things as well as serve as a role model, companion, guide, and confidant (Greenberger, Chen and Beam, 1998).

Cruz's mentorship of Violet was the only instance of extended family serving as mentors. Levine and Munsch (2011) define mentorship as "a formal relationship in which a nonparental adult provides a range of functions to a younger person, or a naturally occurring relationship that provides the same function" (Pg. 455). As discussed in the previous chapter on parents, a number of secret-identity tween sitcom parents acted as teachers and role models in characters' secret lives (Miley's father on *Hannah Montana*, Hank and Bob Thunderman on *The Thundermans*, Vic and Eva Madden on *The Villains of Valley View*, Donald Davenport on *Lab Rats*, Aunt Hilda and Aunt Zelda on *Sabrina the Teenage Witch*, Jerry Russo on *Wizards of Waverly Place*, and Kira and Craig Cooper on *K.C. Undercover*). However, it is important to mention the two shows that had non-family members serving as mentors: *Mighty Med* and *Henry Danger*.

In *Mighty Med*, Dr. Horace Diaz serves as employer and mentor to the main characters, Kaz and Oliver. Horace is characterized as being somewhat eccentric and a little goofy, but when it comes to healing and dealing with supervillains, he is very serious. He cares deeply for his nephew, Alan, and also treats Skylar as a daughter. He always puts the safety of his family and the hospital as his top priority. Horace hires Oliver and Kaz because of their extensive knowledge of superheroes and trains them to be healers at Mighty Med. Horace's mentorship of Oliver and Kaz is more implied than shown. He works with them, but there are not many explicit encounters of him explaining how to be a good healer. He leads more through his example and by letting Oliver and Kaz learn through practice.

Similarly, in *Henry Danger*, Captain Man/Ray serves as mentor to Kid Danger/Henry. He also leads through example and has Henry learn "on the job." While their relationship begins more as a boss/employee, by the end of five seasons, it is obvious that Ray views Henry as a friend and vice versa. They definitely endure some conflict, particularly when Henry shares his secret with his friends and sister. Ray and Henry have a relationship outside of being superheroes, because Ray serves as Henry's boss at Junk-n'Stuff (since their superhero hideout is hidden there). In Season 2, Episode 2 "One Henry, Three Girls: Part 1" Ray lectures Henry about responsibility, and in the following episode we see them training together. In that same episode we see how much Ray cares about Henry when he worries that someone kidnapped Kid Danger.

As Henry matures, their relationship evolves as well. Since they've been a team for so long, there is not as much for Ray to teach Henry. Henry wants to be seen by Ray as more of an equal than a sidekick. This leads to some tension between the two. This tension builds to a climax in Season 5, Episode 36 "The Beginning of the End." Kid Danger is offered a job to be the superhero for Neighborville. He is offered a Danger Cave, his own cheerleaders, his own sidekick, Lil' Dynomite, and his own statue to take the job. Ray gets jealous and confronts Henry, "Maybe you should take the job … ." Henry responds, "I don't want the job." Ray counters, "Oh really, because I'm beginning to question your commitment to Swellview." Henry is shocked and hurt, "My commitment to Swellview, are you kidding me." Ray admits his real feelings, "Well, you don't seem very committed to me." Ray mocks him saying, "Oh my friends are leaving. I'm stuck here in Swellview being a sidekick and saving lives." Henry's feelings finally come boiling up, "Exactly. I've been too busy saving everyone else's life I forgot to have one of my own." Ray reminds him, "You swore an oath to defend this city." Henry responds, "When I was 13. Maybe I don't want to do it anymore." Ray gets mad and emotional, "Because you are obviously scared of being stuck here in Swellview with me." Henry answers, "Yeah, Ray. I don't want to be your sidekick for another 30 or 40 or 50 years." Ray tells him, "Man, that was always the plan. You'd be my sidekick and you'd take over as Captain Man when I retire." Henry hits Ray where it hurts, "I don't want to be Captain Man. I will never, ever be Captain Man." Ray questions him, "Then why are you even here?" To this Henry responds,

"That's a good question." He takes one last gumball and chews it to transform back to Henry. Ray asks, "What are you doing." Henry answers "Quitting" and transforms into Henry and walks out.

This sets up the events for the series finale. Eventually, Ray and Henry make up and repair their friendship and team up to fight Ray's old sidekick, Drex. While they teamed up for this one last mission, they don't stay together as a team. Henry forms his own team with Jasper and Charlotte, while Ray opens SWAG (Swellview Academy for the Gifted) to train a new generation of superheroes. The last words we hear Henry say to Ray are, "See you at Thanksgiving?" Ray answers, "Of course." Even though they are no longer partners, they are even more than friends; they are family.

Since Henry Danger lasted for five seasons we are able to see the progression of this mentorship relationship from beginning to end and the various challenges in between. For shows that had longer runs, there were times when the main characters became mentors themselves. On the fourth season of *Sabrina the Teenage Witch*, Sabrina began to mentor a young witch, Dreama. On the fourth season of *Lab Rats*, the Davenports open the Bionic Academy to train others. Allen and Land (1999) suggest that mentoring shapes the transition into adulthood and helps adolescents accept personal responsibility, make independent decisions, develop a sense of efficacy and individuation, and develop the capacity for mature intimacy.

No matter who is serving as mentor or role model – a nonparental adult, an extended family member, or a parent – the importance of influence of adults in the lives of the main characters on secret-identity tween sitcoms is evident. None of these programs simply focus on these characters themselves; they all include family. A dominant theme of these programs is that family comes first. Families support one another, and together they can take on anything.

References

Allen, Joseph P. and Land, Deborah. 1999. "Attachment in adolescence" In J. Cassidy and P.R. Shaver (Eds.) *Handbook of attachment: Theory, Research, and Clinical Applications*. 319–335, The Guilford Press.

Scales, P.C. and Giboons, J.L. (1996) "Extended Family Members and Unrelated Adults in the Lives of Young Adolescents: A Research Agenda." *The Journal of Early Adolescence*, *16* (4) 365–389.

Greenberger, Ellen, Chen, Chuansheng, and Beam, Margaret R. 1998. The Role of 'Very Important' Nonparental Adults in Adolescent Development. *Journal of Youth and Adolescence*, *27* (3) 321–341.

Levine, Laura and Munsch, Joyce. 2011. *Child Development: An Active Learning Approach*. Washington DC: Sage.

11 Revelation

In Chapter 3, we introduced the secret-identity trope and explained that during the self-exploration period of adolescences, secret-identity stories allow young people to explore possible selves. As a reminder, Markus and Nurius (1986) explained that possible selves allow us to explore who we are, who we want to be, and who we fear to be. In Chapter 5, we also introduced the concept of an AIC (Assor, 2012). Our AIC informs us what is truly important to us, and what we really value and need. Possible selves and AIC only tell part of the self-exploration story, however.

Carl Rogers's (1959) humanistic, person-centered approach to psychology suggests that people want to feel, experience, and behave in ways which are consistent with our *self-image* and which reflect what we would like to be like, our *ideal self*. The closer our self-image and ideal-self are to each other, the more consistent or congruent we are and the higher our sense of self-worth. This congruency of self-image and ideal self suggests that after a period of self-exploration, we do come to a decision of who we want to be (ideal self). It is not surprising, then, that at the conclusion of most of these series, those characters who are leading double lives with a secret identity choose to reconcile the two sides of their identity and share their truth with others. To conclude our exploration of secret-identity tween-sitcoms, we will consider if and how the main secret-identity characters shared their truths with others, and the possible lessons these revelations might teach tween viewers.

The two most recent programs, *Ultra-Violet & Black Scorpion* and *The Villains of Valley View*, did not reach a point where the characters revealed themselves fully. As mentioned in previous chapters, Ultra-Violet originally wanted to tell the world who she was, and her mentor/uncle convinced her that superheroes were supposed to keep their identities hidden. It is interesting to note that as Violet is just 13, she is entering into the heart of adolescence. This is a time when social comparison is at its peak. The fact that she at first embraced her true self and then had to hide it could symbolically represent what happens to many people as they are in middle school and about to enter high school. Are they confident in who

DOI: 10.4324/9781003593027-11

they are? What forces are convincing them to hide parts of themselves from others? Since *Ultra-Violet & Black Scorpion* was canceled, we will not learn her full journey of self-identity.

The Villains of Valley View was renewed for a second season, so audiences will be able to continue their journey with Maddens. As a reminder from previous chapters, in the Season 1 finale the Maddens came full circle, embracing living life in Valley View and realizing that their old villain life didn't feel like them anymore. But audiences were left with the cliff-hanger that Amy Madden was now the head of all supervillains, since she defeated Onyx. This sets up an interesting storyline for the show's second season. How will Amy and the Madden's handle the temptations of power? They no longer need to hide from the other supervillains. What will they ultimately decide to do? They will need to figure out their authentic selves, and will likely be tested in the process.

The show that had the longest story and character arc was *Sabrina the Teenage Witch*. Her story could actually be looked at in two ways. Originally, the show was set to end after four seasons on ABC, as Sabrina completed high school. But the show was moved to The WB and retooled to fit Sabrina's life at college (which was shortened to 2 years) and then post college for the actual final season. In the chapter on romance, we explored Sabrina's relationship with her soulmate Harvey and how at the end of Season 4 he figured out that she was a witch. But because of the retooling, she did not end up back together with Harvey until the very last episode of the season. Besides the soulmate story, the other long-term theme that *Sabrina the Teenage Witch* potentially teaches audiences is to embrace your true self. Besides Harvey, Sabrina never revealed that she was a witch to any other mortal. But over the course of the series, Sabrina learned to accept and ultimately appreciate that she was different.

Henry Danger ran for five seasons. Henry's story gives audiences an opportunity to explore Henry Hart's secret-life journey from start to finish. Henry was just 13 years old when he became Captain Man's sidekick, Kid Danger. Early on he shared his secret with his best friends, Charlotte and Jasper. It wasn't until the final season that Henry shared his identity with his family, first his sister and finally his parents. The previous chapter on mentor relationships explained the choice Henry made to leave Captain Man and go off on his own. Henry needed to become his own person, rather than someone's sidekick. His closest relationships continued to be Charlotte and Jasper, and they form their own team. Still, he retains his relationship with his family and Captain Man; they have just redefined their relationships as Henry grew into a young man who needed to live his own life on his own terms. This mirrors typical adolescence.

Miley Stewart's journey to revealing that she was Hannah Montana was discussed in both the chapters on friendship and romance. Like Henry Hart, Miley Stewart was just 13 when she made the decision to have a separate persona for her music career. She wanted to live a normal life. Though she wanted to be normal, in the end she needed to accept and embrace that she was different. The longer and harder she tried to hide who she really was, the more trouble it created, especially in her closest relationships. This is a lesson that any young person could learn from. While much of adolescence involves social comparison and the need to fit in, they will ultimately be most content when they reconcile their self-image with their ideal self. Like most of the morals found in *Hannah Montana*, the lyrics of the songs sum things up perfectly. As Miley made the decision to let go of Hanna Montana, the song "Wherever I Go" played. It was Miley's goodbye to Hanna:

> Oh yeah
> Here we are now
> Everything is about to change
> We face tomorrow
> As we say goodbye to yesterday
> A chapter ending but the stories only just begun
> A page is turning for everyone
> So I'm moving on, letting go
> Holding on to tomorrow
> I've always got
> The memories while I'm finding out who I'm gonna be
> We might be apart but I hope you always know
> You'll be with me wherever I go
> Wherever I go
> So excited I can barely even catch my breath
> We have each other to lean on for the road ahead
> This happy ending is the start of all our dreams
> And I know your heart is with me
> So I'm moving on, letting go
> Holding on to tomorrow
> I've always got
> The memories while I'm finding out who I'm gonna be
> We might be apart but I hope you always know
> You'll be with me wherever I go
> It's time to show the world we've got something to say
> A song to sing out loud we'll never fade away
> I know I'll miss you but we'll meet again someday
> We'll never fade away
> So I'm moving on, letting go
> Holding on to tomorrow
> I've always got
> The memories while I'm finding out who I'm gonna be

We might be apart but I hope you always know
You'll be with me wherever I go
So I'm moving on, letting go
Holding on to tomorrow
I've always got
The memories while I'm finding out who I'm gonna be
We might be apart but I hope you always know
You'll be with me
Yeah
Wherever I go
Wherever I
Wherever I go

Source: LyricFindSong
writers: Adam Watts / Andrew Creighton Dodd

As the chorus explains, she'll always have the memories of Hannah Montana, but she needs to figure out who she is as Miley. But Hannah will be a part of her wherever she goes.

On *Lab Rats*, Season 3, Episode 13 "You Posted What" the bionic Davenport siblings are caught on video using their bionics and the video goes viral, revealing their secret to the world. Government agents swarm their house and place Davenport and the Lab Rats on lock-down. With the government is now having knowledge of the bionic secret, they try to gain control of the siblings, through separation from Davenport. Eventually the team is reunited, but now that their secret has been revealed the family dynamic has changed a bit. Though they didn't make the conscious decision to "out" themselves, once they are out in the open it allows them to help more people. They decide to open the Bionic Academy to train others. The implicit lesson here could be that if others learn about our true selves before we are ready to share, they may in fact be doing us a favor and letting us be our authentic selves.

The superhero world of *Mighty Med* was never revealed to the public, so Kaz and Oliver's secret identity story arc was not one of revelation, but more of transformation. Only when Oliver realized that his mom was actually Mr. Terror and she left, was he able to gain his own superpowers. It could be implied that his mother was holding him back from becoming his true, authentic self.

In *Wizards of Waverly Place*, audiences think that the Russos reveal the wizarding world to the public in Season 3, Episode 29 "Wizards Exposed" only to learn that it was a test that the Russos failed. The Russos thought they revealed the wizarding world to save wizards who were being unlawfully detained by the government. But since it was only a test, and they failed, the siblings are demoted in their wizarding levels and have to wait even longer to compete in the family wizard competition. After that, none of the Russos divulge the wizarding secret ever again. They protect the secret. The only mortals that know, besides their parents, are Harper and her boyfriend Zeke. The "false alarm" revelation to the outside world could be a warning to audiences to make sure that your choice to reveal your true self could have repercussions beyond yourself, whether you intend them to or not. That is not to say that because of that you should NOT reveal your authentic self, but just to be mindful and share it with those closest to you first.

One character who does not technically reveal herself to the outside world is K.C. on *K.C. Undercover*. Since K.C. is a spy, she'd be putting a lot of people in danger if she revealed the truth. Still, at the end of the series, K.C. is graduating high school and is struggling to decide if she wants to go to college or if she wants to continue being a spy. K.C. is supposed to deliver the commencement speech, since she is valedictorian, but she is struggling to write it. At the ceremony, her two worlds collide, as double agents infiltrate her school and attack K.C. and her family. They fight them off of course, and since K.C. knows that they are going to have to wipe the memory of her classmates and the rest of the audience, she lets herself speak her truth.

> Here's the deal. A lot of you are probably wondering why I never went to parties, or joined the chess club, or the mathletes. That's because I've been kind of busy, saving the world. For the past three years I have been leading a double life as a teenage spy. You guys have no idea what it's like having to live a lie, constantly having to go undercover as someone else when I don't even know who I am yet. You know, I'm not going to lie, it's been hard … really, really hard. And I've been struggling with this speech, because, how I am supposed to give you guys advice about the future when I haven't even decided what mine is yet. I thought that I had to continue to be a spy, because that's what I am. I am a spy. But then I was like, but I also work really hard in school and I deserve to go to college. And up until like five minutes ago, that's what I was gonna do. But, what just happened here, changed my mind. Again. And now, I'm 100% sure about my decision. I'm gonna be a spy. AND I'm going to college. I'm going to do both, because that's what I've done all along. And it hasn't always been easy, and it hasn't always been perfect, but I think if you believe in yourself you can have it all. And you know what, you should at least try to. If you remember anything today, remember that. Try to have it all.

There is a bigger lesson here besides K.C.'s explicit advice to "Try to have it all." Even though no one in the audience remembered her speech, besides her friend Marisa and her family, she was really speaking to herself. The message here is that it doesn't matter who knows about the different aspects of your life. Ultimately, you need to be honest with yourself and do what is best for you.

The final show to mention is *The Thundermans*. In the chapter about siblings, we learn that at the end of the series, Phoebe and Max's twin power defeats the villain and results in their recruitment to lead the Z-force and enlist the rest of their family to work with them. Phoebe's conclusion bears repeating here, "You guys gave up being superheroes so we could have a normal life. But maybe being a family of superheroes is our normal life." The underlying message here is similar to what was seen in some of the earlier programs. Rather than trying to blend in and be normal, the Thundermans needed to embrace what made them exceptional. By embracing that, they could literally save the world.

Final Thoughts

Through looking at the lives of the young characters on secret-identity tween sitcoms, their experiences, and their relationships, three central themes emerge: (1) true friends are special and always deserve the truth; (2) family always comes first and families always support one another; and (3) embrace your authentic self. Don't try too hard to blend in. Celebrate what makes you, YOU.

References

Assor, Avi. 2012. "Allowing choice and nurturing an inner compass: Educational practices supporting students' need for autonomy." In Christenson, S. Reschly, A. and Wylie, C. (eds.) *Handbook of research on student engagement*. 421–439. Boston, MA.

Markus, Hazel and Nurius, Paula. 1986. "Possible Selves." *American Psychologist 41* (9) 954–969.

Roger, Carl. 1959. "A Theory of Therapy, Personality and Interpersonal Relationships as Developed in the Client-centered Framework." *Journal of Consulting and Clinical Psychology*, *21*, 95–103.

Appendix

Program Details of Secret-Identity Tween Sitcoms in order of earliest broadcast premiere

Sabrina the Teenage Witch

Originally Broadcast on ABC (Seasons 1–4) and then The WB (Seasons 5–7)

Streaming on Hulu

- Creators
  - Jonathan Schmock
  - Nell Scovell
- Production Company:
  - Finishing The Hat (1996)
  - Hartbreak Films
  - Viacom Productions
  - Archie Comics Publications
  - Paramount Network Television
- Main Cast (in credited order)
  - Melissa Joan Hart as Sabrina Spellman
  - Nick Bakay as Salem Saberhagen
  - Caroline Rhea as Hilda Spellman
  - Beth Broderick as Zelda Spellman
  - Nate Richert as Harvey Kinkle
  - Jenna Leigh Green as Libby Chessler
  - Lindsay Sloan as Valerie Birkhead
  - Michelle Beaudoin as Jenny Kelley
  - China Shavers as Dreama
  - Soleil Moon Frye as Roxy King
  - Elisa Donovan as Morgan Cavanaugh
  - David Lascher as Josh
  - Penn Jillette as Drell

- Episode Names and Original Broadcast Dates
    - Season 1 – Broadcast on ABC
        - Episode 1 "Pilot" originally broadcast September 27, 1996
        - Episode 2 "Bundt Friday" originally broadcast October 4, 1996
        - Episode 3 "The True Adventures of Rudy Kazootie" originally broadcast October 11, 1996
        - Episode 4 "Terrible Things" originally broadcast October 18, 1996
        - Episode 5 "A Halloween Story" originally broadcast October 25, 1996
        - Episode 6 " Dream Date" originally broadcast November 1, 1996
        - Episode 7 "Third Aunt from the Sun" originally broadcast November 8, 1996
        - Episode 8 "Magic Joel" originally broadcast November 15, 1996
        - Episode 9 "Geek Like Me" originally broadcast November 22, 1996
        - Episode 10 "Sweet and Sour Victory" originally broadcast December 6, 1996
        - Episode 11 "A Girl and Her Cat" originally broadcast December 13, 1996
        - Episode 12 "Trial by Fury" originally broadcast January 3, 1997
        - Episode 13 "Jenny's Non-Dream" originally broadcast January 10, 1997
        - Episode 14 "Sabrina Through the Looking Glass" originally broadcast January 17, 1997
        - Episode 15 "Hilda and Zelda: The Teenage Years" originally broadcast January 31, 1997
        - Episode 16 "Mars Attracts!" originally broadcast February 7, 1997
        - Episode 17 "First Kiss" originally broadcast February 14, 1997
        - Episode 18 "Sweet Charity" originally broadcast March 7, 1997
        - Episode 19 "Cat Showdown" originally broadcast March 21, 1997
        - Episode 20 "Meeting Dad's Girlfriend" originally broadcast April 4, 1997
        - Episode 21 "As Westbridge Turns" originally broadcast April 25, 1997
        - Episode 22 "The Great Mistake" originally broadcast May 2, 1997
        - Episode 23 "The Crucible" originally broadcast May 9, 1997
        - Episode 24 "Troll Bride" originally broadcast May 16, 1997

- Season 2
  - Episode 1 "Sabrina Gets Her License: Part 1" originally broadcast September 26, 1997
  - Episode 2 "Sabrina Gets Her License: Part 2" originally broadcast September 26, 1997
  - Episode 3 "Dummy for Love" originally broadcast October 3, 1997
  - Episode 4 "Dante's Inferno" originally broadcast October 10, 1997
  - Episode 5 "A Doll's Story" originally broadcast October 17, 1997
  - Episode 6 "Sabrina, the Teenage Boy" originally broadcast October 24, 1997
  - Episode 7 "A River of Candy Corn Runs Through It" originally broadcast October 31, 1997
  - Episode 8 "Inna Gadda Sabrina" originally broadcast November 7, 1997
  - Episode 9 "Witch Trash" originally broadcast November 14, 1997
  - Episode 10"To Tell a Mortal" originally broadcast November 21, 1997
  - Episode 11 "Oh What a Tangled Spell She Weaves" originally broadcast December 5, 1997
  - Episode 12 "Sabrina Claus" originally broadcast December 19, 1997
  - Episode 13 "Little Big Kraft" originally broadcast January 9, 1998
  - Episode 14 "Five Easy Pieces of Libby" originally broadcast January 23, 1998
  - Episode 15 "Finger Lickin' Flu" originally broadcast January 30, 1998
  - Episode 16 "Sabrina and the Beanstalk" originally broadcast February 6, 1998
  - Episode 17 "The Equalizer" originally broadcast February 13, 1998
  - Episode 18 "The Band Episode" originally broadcast February 28, 1998
  - Episode 19 "When Teens Collide" originally broadcast March 6, 1998
  - Episode 20 "My Nightmare, the Car" originally broadcast March 20, 1998
  - Episode 21 "Fear Strikes Up a Conversation" originally broadcast April 3, 1998

    - Episode 22 "Quiz Show" originally broadcast April 17, 1998
    - Episode 23 "Disneyworld" originally broadcast April 24, 1998
    - Episode 24 "Sabrina's Choice" originally broadcast May 1, 1998
    - Episode 25 "Rumor Mill" originally broadcast May 8, 1998
    - Episode 26 "Mom vs. Magic" originally broadcast May 15, 1998

- Season 3

    - Episode 1 "It's a Mad Mad Mad Mad Season Opener" originally broadcast September 25, 1998
    - Episode 2 "Boy Was my Face Red" originally broadcast October 2, 1998
    - Episode 3 "Suspicious Minds" originally broadcast October 9, 1998
    - Episode 4 "The Pom Pom Incident" originally broadcast October 16, 1998
    - Episode 5 "Pancake Madness" originally broadcast October 23, 1998
    - Episode 6 "Good Will Haunting" originally broadcast October 30, 1998
    - Episode 7 "You Bet Your Family" originally broadcast November 6, 1998
    - Episode 8 "And the Sabrina Goes To…" originally broadcast November 13, 1998
    - Episode 9 "Nobody Nose Libby Like Sabrina Nose Libby" originally broadcast November 20, 1998
    - Episode 10 "Sabrina and the Beast" originally broadcast November 27, 1998
    - Episode 11 "Christmas Amnesia" originally broadcast December 11, 1998
    - Episode 12 "Whose So-Called Life Is It Anyway?" originally broadcast January 8, 1999
    - Episode 13 "What Price Harvey?" originally broadcast January 15, 1999
    - Episode 14 "Mrs. Kraft" originally broadcast January 29, 1999
    - Episode 15 "Sabrina and the Pirates" originally broadcast February 5, 1999
    - Episode 16 "Sabrina, the Matchmaker" originally broadcast February 12, 1999
    - Episode 17 "Salem, the Boy" originally broadcast February 19, 1999
    - Episode 18 "Sabrina, The Teenage Writer" originally broadcast February 26, 1999
    - Episode 19 "The Big Sleep" originally broadcast March 12, 1999

- Episode 20 "Sabrina's Pen Pal" originally broadcast March 26, 1999
- Episode 21 "Sabrina's Real World" originally broadcast April 9, 1999
- Episode 22 "The Long and Winding Shortcut" originally broadcast April 9, 1999
- Episode 23 "Sabrina, the Sandman" originally broadcast May 7, 1999
- Episode 24 "Silent Movie" originally broadcast May 14, 1999
- Episode 25 "The Good, the Bad, and the Luau" originally broadcast May 21, 1999

- Season 4
  - Episode 1 "No Place Like Home" originally broadcast September 24, 1999
  - Episode 2 "Dream a Little Dreama Me" originally broadcast October 1, 1999
  - Episode 3 "Jealousy" originally broadcast October 8, 1999
  - Episode 4 "Jealousy: Little Orphan Hilda Part 2" originally broadcast October 15, 1999
  - Episode 5 "Spoiled Rotten" originally broadcast October 22, 1999
  - Episode 6 "Episode LXXXI: The Phantom Menace" originally broadcast October 29, 1999
  - Episode 7 "Prelude to a Kiss" originally broadcast November 5, 1999
  - Episode 8 "Aging, Not So Gracefully" originally broadcast November 12, 1999
  - Episode 9 "Love Means Having to Say You're Sorry" originally broadcast November 19, 1999
  - Episode 10 "Ice Station Sabrina" originally broadcast November 21, 1999
  - Episode 11 "Salem and Juliette" originally broadcast December 199, 1999
  - Episode 12 "Sabrina, Nipping at Your Nose" originally broadcast December 17, 1999
  - Episode 13 "Now You See Her, Now You Don't" originally broadcast January 7, 2000
  - Episode 14 "Super Hero" originally broadcast January 21, 2000
  - Episode 15 "Love in Bloom" originally broadcast February 11, 2000
  - Episode 16 "Welcome Back, Duke" originally broadcast February 25, 2000

- Episode 17 "Salem's Daughter" originally broadcast March 3, 2000
- Episode 18 "Dreama, the Mouse" originally broadcast March 17, 2000
- Episode 19 "The Wild, Wild Witch" originally broadcast March 31, 2000
- Episode 20 "She's Baaaack!" originally broadcast April 14, 2000
- Episode 21 "The Four Faces of Sabrina" originally broadcast April 28, 2000
- Episode 22 "The End of an Era" originally broadcast May 5, 2000

- Season 5
  - Episode 1 "Every Witch Way but Loose" originally broadcast September 22, 2000.
  - Episode 2 "Double-Time" originally broadcast September 29, 2000
  - Episode 3 "Heart of the Matter" originally broadcast October 6, 2000
  - Episode 4 "You Can't Win" originally broadcast October 13, 2000
  - Episode 5 "House of PI's" originally broadcast October 20, 2000
  - Episode 6 "The Halloween Scene" originally broadcast October 27, 2000
  - Episode 7 "Welcome Traveler" originally broadcast November 3, 2000
  - Episode 8 "Some of My Best Friends Are Half Mortals" originally broadcast November 10, 2000
  - Episode 9 "Lost at C" originally broadcast November 17, 2000
  - Episode 10 "Sabrina's Perfect Christmas" originally broadcast December 15, 2000
  - Episode 11 "My Best Shot" originally broadcast January 12, 2001
  - Episode 12 "Tick-Tock Hilda's Clock" originally broadcast January 19, 2001
  - Episode 13 "Sabrina's New Roommate" originally broadcast January 26, 2001
  - Episode 14 "Making the Grade" originally broadcast February 2, 2001
  - Episode 15 "Love Is a Many Complicated Thing" originally broadcast February 9, 2001
  - Episode 16 "Sabrina, The Muse" originally broadcast February 16, 2001

  - Episode 17 "Beach Blanket Bizarro" originally broadcast February 23, 2001
  - Episode 18 "Witchright Hall" originally broadcast April 6, 2001
  - Episode 19 "Sabrina, the Activist" originally broadcast April 27, 2001
  - Episode 20 "Do You See What I See?" originally broadcast May 4, 2001
  - Episode 21 "Sabrina's Got Spirit" originally broadcast May 11, 2001
  - Episode 22 "Finally" originally broadcast May 18, 2001

- Season 6

  - Episode 1 "Really Big Season Opener" originally broadcast October 5, 2001
  - Episode 2 "Sabrina's Date with Destiny" originally broadcast October 12, 2001
  - Episode 3 "What's News" originally broadcast October 19, 2001
  - Episode 4 "Murder on the Halloween Express" originally broadcast October 26, 2001
  - Episode 5 "The Gift of Gab" originally broadcast
  - Episode 6 "Thin Ice" originally broadcast November 9, 2001
  - Episode 7 "Hex, Lies and No Video Tape" Thin Ice" originally broadcast November 16, 2001
  - Episode 8 "Humble Pie" originally broadcast December 7, 2001
  - Episode 9 "A Birthday Witch" originally broadcast December 7, 2001
  - Episode 10 "Deliver Us From E-Mail" originally broadcast January 19, 2002
  - Episode 11 "Cloud Ten" originally broadcast January 25, 2002
  - Episode 12 "Sabrina and the Candidate" originally broadcast February 1, 2002
  - Episode 13 "I Think I Love You" originally broadcast February 15, 2002
  - Episode 14 "The Arrangement" originally broadcast February 22, 2022
  - Episode 15 "Time After Time" originally broadcast March 15, 2002
  - Episode 16 "Sabrina and the Kids" originally broadcast March 22, 2002
  - Episode 17 "The Competition" originally broadcast April 5, 2002
  - Episode 18 "I, Busybody" originally broadcast April 12, 2002
  - Episode 19 "Guilty" originally broadcast April 19, 2002

- Episode 20 "The Whole Ball of Wax" originally broadcast April 26, 2002
- Episode 21 "Driving Mr. Goodman" originally broadcast May 3, 2002
- Episode 22 "I Fall to Pieces" originally broadcast May 10, 2002

- Season 7
  - Episode 1 "Total Sabrina Live" originally broadcast September 20, 2002
  - Episode 2 "The Big Head" originally broadcast September 27, 2002
  - Episode 3 "Call Me Crazy" originally broadcast October 4, 2002
  - Episode 4 "Shift Happens" originally broadcast October 11, 2002
  - Episode 5 "Free Sabrina" originally broadcast October 18, 2002
  - Episode 6 "Sabrina Unplugged" originally broadcast November 1, 2002
  - Episode 7 "Witch Way Out" originally broadcast November 1, 2002
  - Episode 8 "Bada-Ping" originally broadcast November 15, 2002
  - Episode 9 "It's a Hot, Hot, Hot, Hot Christmas" originally broadcast December 6, 2002
  - Episode 10, "Ping, Ping a Song" originally broadcast January 10, 2003
  - Episode 11 "The Lyin', the Witch and the Wardrobe" originally broadcast January 17, 2003
  - Episode 12 "In Sabrina We Trust" originally broadcast January 24, 2003
  - Episode 13 "Sabrina in Wonderland" originally broadcast January 31, 2003
  - Episode 14 "Present Perfect" originally broadcast February 7, 2003
  - Episode 15 "Cirque du Sabrina" originally broadcast February 14, 2003
  - Episode 16 "Getting to Nose You" originally broadcast February 21, 2003
  - Episode 17 "Romance Looming" originally broadcast February 27, 2003
  - Episode 18 "Spellmanian Slip" originally broadcast March 20, 2003
  - Episode 19 "You Slay Me" originally broadcast March 27, 2003
  - Episode 20 "A Fish Tale" originally broadcast April 17, 2003
  - Episode 21 "What a Witch Wants" originally broadcast April 24, 2003
  - Episode 22 "Soul Mates" originally broadcast April 24, 2003

Hannah Montana

Originally Broadcast on Disney Channel
Streaming on Disney+

- Creators
  - Richard Correll
  - Barry O'Brien
  - Michael Poryes
- Production Company
  - It's a Laugh Productions
  - Michael Poryes Productions
  - Disney Channel
- Main Cast (in credited order)
  - Miley Cyrus as Miley Stewart/Hannah Montana
  - Emily Osment as Lilly Truscott
  - Jason Earls as Jackson Stewart
  - Billy Ray Cyrus as Robby Ray Stewart
  - Mitchel Musso as Oliver Oken
  - Moises Arias as Rico
  - Cody Linley as Jake Ryan
- Episode Names and Original Broadcast Dates
  - Season 1
    - Episode 1 "Lilly, Do You Want to Know a Secret?" originally broadcast March 24, 2006
    - Episode 2 "Miley Get Your Gum" originally broadcast March 31, 2006
    - Episode 3 "She's a Supersneak" originally broadcast April 7, 2006
    - Episode 4 "I Can't Make You Love Hannah if You Don't" originally broadcast April 14, 2006
    - Episode 5 "It's My Party and I'll Lie if I Want To" originally broadcast April 21, 2006
    - Episode 6 "Grandmas Don't Let Your Babies Grow Up to Play Favorites" originally broadcast April 28, 2006
    - Episode 7 "It's a Mannequin's World" originally broadcast May 12, 2006
    - Episode 8 "Mascot Love" originally broadcast May 12, 2006
    - Episode 9 " Ooo, Ooo, Itchy Woman" originally broadcast June 10, 2006

- Episode 10 "O Say, Can You Remember the Words?" originally broadcast June 30, 2006
- Episode 11 "Oops! I Meddled Again!" originally broadcast July 15, 2006
- Episode 12 "On the Road Again?" originally broadcast July 28, 2006
- Episode 13 "You're So Vain, You Probably Think This Zit is About You" originally broadcast August 12, 2006
- Episode 14 "New Kid in School" originally broadcast August 18, 2006
- Episode 15 "More Tan a Zombie to Me" originally broadcast September 8, 2006
- Episode 16 "Good Golly, Miss Molly" originally broadcast September 29, 2006
- Episode 17 "Torn Between Two Hannahs" originally broadcast October 14, 2006
- Episode 18 "People Who Use People" originally broadcast November 2006
- Episode 19 "Money for Nothing, Guilt for Free" originally broadcast November 26, 2006
- Episode 20 "Debt it Be" originally broadcast December 1, 2006
- Episode 21 "My Boyfriend's Jackson and There's Gonna Be Trouble" originally broadcast December 31, 2006
- Episode 22 "We Are Family: Now Get Me Some Water!" originally broadcast January 7, 2007
- Episode 23 "Schooly Bully" originally broadcast January 19, 2007
- Episode 24 "The Idol Side of Me" originally broadcast February 9, 2007
- Episode 25 "Smells Like Teen Sellout" originally broadcast March 2, 2007

- Season 2
  - Episode 1 "Me and Rico Down by the School Yard" originally broadcast April 23, 2007
  - Episode 2 "Cuffs Will Keep Us Together" originally broadcast April 24, 2007
  - Episode 3 "You Are So Sue-able to Me" originally broadcast April 25, 2007
  - Episode 4 "Get Down Study-udy-udy" originally broadcast April 26, 2007
  - Episode 5 "I am Hannah Hear Me Crock" originally broadcast April 27, 2007

- Episode 6 "You Gotta Not Fight For Your Right To Party" originally broadcast April 27, 2007
- Episode 7 "My Best Friend's Boyfriend" originally broadcast May 18, 2007
- Episode 8 "Take This Job and Love It" originally broadcast June 16, 2007
- Episode 9 "Achy Jakey Heart: Part 1" originally broadcast June 24, 2007
- Episode 10 "Achy Jakey Heart: Part 2" originally broadcast June 24, 2007
- Episode 11 "Sleepwalk This Way" originally broadcast July 7, 2007
- Episode 12 "When You Wish You Were the Star" originally broadcast July 13, 2007
- Episode 13 "I Want You to Want Me…to Go to Florida" originally broadcast July 21, 2007
- Episode 14 "Everybody Was Best Friend Fighting" originally broadcast July 29, 2007
- Episode 15 "Song Sung Bad" originally broadcast August 4, 2007
- Episode 16 "Me and Mr. Jonas and Mr. Jonas and Mr. Jonas" originally broadcast August 17, 2007
- Episode 17, "Don't Stop Till You Get the Phone" originally broadcast September 21, 2007
- Episode 18 "That's What Friends Are For?" originally broadcast October 19, 2007
- Episode 19 "Lilly's Mom Has Got It Goin' On" originally broadcast November 10, 2007
- Episode 20 "I Will Always Loathe You" originally broadcast December 7, 2007
- Episode 21 "Bye Bye Ball" originally broadcast January 13, 2008
- Episode 22 "(We're So Sorry) Uncle Earl" originally broadcast March 21, 2008
- Episode 23 "The Way We Almost Weren't" originally broadcast May 4, 2008
- Episode 24 "You Didn't Say It's Your Birthday" originally broadcast July 6, 2008
- Episode 25 "Hannah in the Streets With Diamonds" originally broadcast July 20, 2008
- Episode 26 "Yet Another Side of. Me" originally broadcast August 3, 2008
- Episode 27 "Joannie B. Goode" originally broadcast August 31, 2008

  - Episode 28 "The Test of My Love" originally broadcast August 31, 2008
  - Episode 29 "We're All on This Date Together" originally broadcast October 12, 2008

- Season 3

  - Episode 1 "He Ain't a Hottie, He's My Brother" originally broadcast November 2, 2008
  - Episode 2 "Ready, Set, Don't Drive" originally broadcast November 9, 2008
  - Episode 3 "Don't Go Breaking My Tooth" originally broadcast November 16, 2008
  - Episode 4 "You Never Give Me My Money" originally broadcast November 23, 2008
  - Episode 5 "Killing Me Softly With His Height" originally broadcast December 14, 2008
  - Episode 6 "Would I Lie to You, Lilly?" originally broadcast January 11, 2009
  - Episode 7 "You Gotta Lose That Job" originally broadcast February 16, 2009
  - Episode 8 "Welcome to the Bungle" originally broadcast March 1, 2009
  - Episode 9 "Papa's Got a Brand New Friend" originally broadcast March 8, 2009
  - Episode 10 "Cheat It" originally broadcast March 15, 2009
  - Episode 11 "Knock Knock Knockin' on Jackson's Head" originally broadcast March 22, 2009
  - Episode 12 "You Give Lunch a Bad Name" originally broadcast March 29, 2009
  - Episode 13 "What I Don't Like About You" originally broadcast April 17, 2009
  - Episode 14 "Promma Mia" originally broadcast May 3, 2009
  - Episode 15 "Once, Twice, Three Times Afraidy" originally broadcast May 17, 2009
  - Episode 16 "Jake...Another Little Piece of My Heart" originally broadcast June 7, 2009
  - Episode 17 "Miley Hurt the Feelings of the Radio Star" originally broadcast June 14, 2009
  - Episode 18 "He Could Be the One" originally broadcast July 5, 2009
  - Episode 19 "Super(stitious) Girl" originally broadcast July 17, 2009
  - Episode 20 "I Honestly Love You (No, Not You)" originally broadcast July 26, 2009

- Episode 21 "For(Give) a Little Bit" originally broadcast August 9, 2009
- Episode 22 "B-B-B-Bad to the Chrome" originally broadcast September 20, 2009
- Episode 23 "Uptight (Oliver's Alright)" originally broadcast September 20, 2009
- Episode 24 "Judge Me Tender" originally broadcast October 18, 2009
- Episode 25 "Can't Get Home to You, Girl" originally broadcast November 8, 2009
- Episode 26 "Come Fail Away" originally broadcast December 6, 2009
- Episode 27 "Got to Get Her Out of My House" originally broadcast January 10, 2010
- Episode 28 "The Wheel Near My Bed (Keeps on Turnin')" originally broadcast February 21, 2010
- Episode 29 "Miley Says Goodbye – Part 1" originally broadcast March 7, 2010
- Episode 30 "Miley Says Goodbye – Part 2" originally broadcast March 14, 2010

- Season 4

  - Episode 1 "Sweet Home Hannah Montana" originally broadcast July 11, 2010
  - Episode 2 "Hannah Montana to the Principal's Office" originally broadcast July 18, 2010
  - Episode 3 "California Screamin'" originally broadcast July 25, 2010
  - Episode 4 "De-Do-Do-Do, Da-Don't-Don't-Don't Tell My Secret!" originally broadcast August 1, 2010
  - Episode 5 "It's the End of the Jake As We Know It" originally broadcast August 8, 2010
  - Episode 6 "Been Here All Along" originally broadcast August 22, 2010
  - Episode 7 "Love That Lets Go" originally broadcast September 12, 2010
  - Episode 8 "Hannah's Gonna Get This" originally broadcast October 3, 2010
  - Episode 9 "I'll Always Remember You – Part 1" originally broadcast November 7, 2010
  - Episode 10 "I'll Always Remember You – Part 2" originally broadcast November 7, 2010
  - Episode 11 "Kiss It All Goodbye" originally broadcast December 19, 2010

        - Episode 12 "I am Mamaw, Hear Me Roar!" originally broadcast January 9, 2011
        - Episode 13 "Wherever I Go" originally broadcast January 16, 2021

Wizards of Waverly Place
Originally Broadcast on Disney Channel
Streaming on Disney+

- Creator
    - Todd Greenwald
- Production Company
    - It's A Laugh Productions
- Main Cast (in credited order)
    - Selena Gomez as Alex Russo
    - David Henrie as Justin Russo
    - Jake T. Austin as Max Russo
    - Jennifer Stone as Harper Finkle
    - Maria Canals-Barrera as Theresa Russo
    - David DeLuise as Jerry Russo
    - Daniel Benson as Zeke Beakerman
    - Gregg Sulkin as Mason Greyback
    - Bridgit Mendler as Juliet Van Heusen
    - McKaley Miller as Talia
- Episode Names and Original Broadcast Dates
    - Season 1
        - Episode 1 "Crazy Ten-Minute Sale" originally broadcast October 12, 2007
        - Episode 2 "First Kiss" originally broadcast October 18, 2007
        - Episode 3 "I Almost Drowned in a Chocolate Fountain" originally broadcast October 26, 2007
        - Episode 4 "New Employee" originally broadcast November 2, 2007
        - Episode 5 "Disenchanted Evening" originally broadcast November 9, 2007
        - Episode 6 "You Can't Always Get What You Carpet" originally broadcast November 10, 2007
        - Episode 7 "Alex's Choice" originally broadcast November 16, 2007
        - Episode 8 "Curb Your Dragon" originally broadcast November 30, 2007

  - Episode 9 “Movies” originally broadcast December 14, 2007
  - Episode 10 “Pop Me and We Both Go Down” originally broadcast January 6, 2008
  - Episode 11 “Potion Commotion” originally broadcast February 10, 2008
  - Episode 12 “Justin’s Little Sister” originally broadcast March 9, 2008
  - Episode 13 “Wizard School, Part 1” originally broadcast April 6, 2008
  - Episode 14 “Wizard School, Part 2” originally broadcast April 6, 2008
  - Episode 15 “The Supernatural” originally broadcast Mary 18, 2008
  - Episode 16 “Alex in the Middle” originally broadcast June 15, 2008
  - Episode 17 “Report Card” originally broadcast June 29, 2008
  - Episode 18 “Credit Check” originally broadcast July 6, 2008
  - Episode 19 “Alex’s Spring Fling” originally broadcast July 20, 2008
  - Episode 20 “Quinceanera” originally broadcast August 10, 2008
  - Episode 21 “Art Museum Piece” originally broadcast August 31, 2008

- Season 2

  - Episode 1 “Smarty Pants” originally broadcast September 12, 2008
  - Episode 2 “Beware Wolf” originally broadcast September 21, 2008
  - Episode 3 “Graphic Novel” originally broadcast October 5, 2008
  - Episode 4 “Racing” originally broadcast October 12, 2008
  - Episode 5 “Alex’s Brother Maximan” originally broadcast October 19, 2008
  - Episode 6 “Saving Wiz Tech, Part 1” originally broadcast October 26, 2008
  - Episode 7 “Saving Wiz Tech, Part 2” originally broadcast October 26, 2008
  - Episode 8, “Harper Knows” originally broadcast November 23, 2008
  - Episode 9 “Taxi Dance” originally broadcast December 7, 2008
  - Episode 10 “Baby Cupid” originally broadcast December 14, 2008
  - Episode 11 “Make It Happen” originally broadcast December 31, 2008

- Episode 12 "Fairy Tale" originally broadcast January 25, 2008
- Episode 13 "Fashion Week" originally broadcast February 15, 2009
- Episode 14 "Helping Hand" originally broadcast February 16, 2009
- Episode 15"Art Teacher" originally broadcast March 1, 2009
- Episode 16 "Future Harper" originally broadcast March 15, 2009
- Episode 17 "Alex Does Good" originally broadcast April 5, 2009
- Episode 18 "Hugh's Not Normous" originally broadcast April 12, 2009
- Episode 19 "Don't Rain on Justin's Parade – Earth" originally broadcast April 19, 2009
- Episode 20 "Family Game Night" originally broadcast April 26, 2009
- Episode 21 "Justin's New Girlfriend" originally broadcast May 2, 2009
- Episode 22 "My Tutor My Tutor" originally broadcast May 29, 2009
- Episode 23 "Paint by Committee" originally broadcast June 20, 2009
- Episode 24 "Wizard for a Day" originally broadcast July 10, 2009
- Episode 25 "Wizards on Deck with Hannah Montana" originally broadcast July 17, 2009
- Episode 26 "Wizards vs Vampires on Waverly Place" originally broadcast July 24, 2009
- Episode 27 "Wizards vs Vampires: Tasty Bites" originally broadcast July 31, 2009
- Episode 28 "Wizards vs Vampires: Dream Date" originally broadcast August 7, 2009
- Episode 29 "Wizards vs Vampires vs Zombies" originally broadcast August 8, 2009
- Episode 30 "Retest" originally broadcast August 21, 2009

- Season 3

  - Episode 1 "Franken-Girl" originally broadcast October 9, 2009
  - Episode 2 "Halloween" originally broadcast October 16, 2009
  - Episode 3 "Monster Hunter" originally broadcast October 23, 2009
  - Episode 4 "Three Monsters" originally broadcast October 30, 2009
  - Episode 5 "Night at the Lazerama" originally broadcast November 6, 2009

- Episode 6 "Doll House" originally broadcast November 20, 2009
- Episode 7 "Marathoner Harper" originally broadcast December 6, 2009
- Episode 8 "Alex Charms a Boy" originally broadcast January 15, 2010
- Episode 9 "Wizards vs Werewolves – Part 1" originally broadcast January 22, 2010
- Episode 10 "Wizards vs Werewolves – Part 2" originally broadcast January 22, 1010
- Episode 11 "Positive Alex" originally broadcast February 26, 2010
- Episode 12 "Detention Election" originally broadcast March 19, 2010
- Episode 13 "Dude Looks Like Shakira" originally broadcast April 16, 2010
- Episode 14 "Eat to the Beat" originally broadcast April 30, 2010
- Episode 15 "The Third Wheel" originally broadcast April 30, 2010
- Episode 16 "The Good, the Bad, and the Alex" originally broadcast May 7, 2010
- Episode 17 "Western Show" originally broadcast May 14, 2010
- Episode 18 "Alex's Logo" originally broadcast May 21, 2010
- Episode 19 "Dad's Buggin' Out" originally broadcast June 4, 2010
- Episode 20 "Max's Secret Girlfriend" originally broadcast June 11, 2010
- Episode 21 "Alex Russo, Matchmaker?" originally broadcast July 2, 2010
- Episode 22 "Delinquent Justin" originally broadcast July 16, 2010
- Episode 23 "Wizards vs. Finkles" originally broadcast July 23, 2010
- Episode 24 "Captain Jim Bob Sherwood" originally broadcast July 30, 2010
- Episode 25 "All About You-Niverse" originally broadcast August 27, 2010
- Episode 26 "Uncle Ernesto" originally broadcast August 31, 2010
- Episode 27 "Moving On" originally broadcast September 10, 2010
- Episode 28 "Puppy Love" originally broadcast October 1, 2010
- Episode 29 "Wizards Exposed" originally broadcast October 15, 2010

- Season 4
  - Episode 1 "Alex Tells the World" originally broadcast November 12, 2010
  - Episode 2 "Alex Gives Up" originally broadcast November 27, 2010
  - Episode 3 "Lucky Charmed" originally broadcast December 10, 2010
  - Episode 4 "Journey to the Center of Mason" originally broadcast December 17, 2010
  - Episode 5 "Three Maxes and a Little Lady" originally broadcast January 7, 2011
  - Episode 6 "Daddy's Little Girl" originally broadcast January 21, 2011
  - Episode 7 "Everything's Rosie for Justin" originally broadcast February 4, 2011
  - Episode 8 "Dancing with Angels" originally broadcast February 11, 2011
  - Episode 9 "Wizards vs Angels – Part 1" originally broadcast February 18, 2011
  - Episode 10 "Wizards vs Angels – Part 2" originally broadcast February 18, 2011
  - Episode 11 "Back to Max" originally broadcast March 11, 2011
  - Episode 12 "Zeke Finds Out" originally broadcast April 8, 2011
  - Episode 13 "Magic Unmasked" originally broadcast May 13, 2011
  - Episode 14 "Meet the Werewolves" originally broadcast June 17, 2011
  - Episode 15 "Beast Tamer" originally broadcast June 24, 2011
  - Episode 16 "Wizard of the Year" originally broadcast July 8, 2011
  - Episode 17 "Misfortune at the Beach" originally broadcast July 24, 2011
  - Episode 18 "Wizards vs Asteroids" originally broadcast August 29, 2011
  - Episode 19 "Justin's Back" originally broadcast August 26, 2011
  - Episode 20 "Alex the Puppetmaster" originally broadcast September 16, 2011
  - Episode 21 "My Two Harpers" originally broadcast September 30, 2011
  - Episode 22 "Wizards of Apartment 13B" originally broadcast October 7, 2011
  - Episode 23 "Ghost Roommate" originally broadcast October 14, 2011

    - Episode 24 "Get Along, Little Zombie" originally broadcast October 21, 2011
    - Episode 25 "Wizards vs Everything" originally broadcast October 28, 2011
    - Episode 26 "Rock Around the Clock" originally broadcast November 4, 2011
    - Episode 27 "Harperella" originally broadcast November 18, 2011
    - Episode 28 "Who Will be the Family Wizard?" originally broadcast January 6, 2012.

Lab Rats

Originally Broadcast on Disney XD
Streaming on Disney+

- Creators
  - Bryan Moore
  - Chris Peterson
- Production Company
  - It's a Laugh Productions
- Main Cast (in credited order)
  - William Brent as Chase Davenport
  - Spencer Boldman as Adam Davenport
  - Kelli Berglund as Bree Davenport
  - Tyrel Jackson Williams as Leo Dooley
  - Hal Sparks as Donald Davenport
  - Maile Flanagan as Principal Perry
  - Angel Parker as Tasha Davenport
  - Jeremy Kent Jackson as Douglas Davenport
  - Madison Pettis as Janelle
- Episode Names and Original Broadcast Dates
  - Season 1
    - Episode 1 "Crush, Chop, and Burn, Part 1" originally broadcast February 27, 2012
    - Episode 2 "Crush, Chop, and Burn, Part 2" originally broadcast February 27, 2012
    - Episode 3 "Commando App" originally broadcast March 5, 2012
    - Episode 4 "Leo's Jam" originally broadcast March 12, 2012

  - Episode 5 "Rats on a Train" originally broadcast March 19, 2012
  - Episode 6 "Exoskeleton vs. Grandma" originally broadcast April 6, 2012
  - Episode 7 "Smart and Smarter" originally broadcast April 23, 2012
  - Episode 8 "Bionic Birthday Fail" originally broadcast May 7, 2012
  - Episode 9 "Death Spiral Smackdown" originally broadcast June 7, 2012
  - Episode 10 "Can I Borrow the Helicopter?" originally broadcast June 14, 2012
  - Episode 11 "Back from the Future" originally broadcast June 21, 2012
  - Episode 12 "Chip Switch" originally broadcast June 28, 2012
  - Episode 13 "Drone Alone" originally broadcast July 5, 2012
  - Episode 14 "Chore Wars" originally broadcast July 12, 2012
  - Episode 15 "Dude, Where's My Lab?" originally broadcast July 16, 2012
  - Episode 16 "Air Leo" originally broadcast October 8, 2012
  - Episode 17 "Night of the Living Virus" originally broadcast October 15, 2012
  - Episode 18 "Mission Invisible" originally broadcast October 22, 2012
  - Episode 19 "Concert in a Can" originally broadcast October 29, 2012
  - Episode 20 "Mission: Space" originally broadcast November 5, 2012

- Season 2

  - Episode 1 "Speed Trapped" originally broadcast February 25, 2013
  - Episode 2 "Spy Fly" originally broadcast March 4, 2013
  - Episode 3 "Missin' the Mission" originally broadcast March 11, 2013
  - Episode 4 "Quarantined" originally broadcast March 18, 2013
  - Episode 5 "Robot Fight Club" originally broadcast March 25, 2013
  - Episode 6 "Bro Down" originally broadcast April 1, 2013
  - Episode 7 "The Rats Strike Back" originally broadcast April 8, 2013
  - Episode 8 "Parallel Universe" originally broadcast June 17, 2013

- Episode 9 "Spike's Got Talent" originally broadcast June 24, 2013
- Episode 10 "Leo vs. Evil" originally broadcast June 24, 2013
- Episode 11 "Hole in One" originally broadcast July 1, 2013
- Episode 12 "Trucked Out" originally broadcast July 8, 2013
- Episode 13 "The Bionic 500" originally broadcast July 22, 2013
- Episode 14 "Bionic Showdown: Part One" originally broadcast August 5, 2013
- Episode 15 "Bionic Showdown: Part Two" originally broadcast August 5, 2013
- Episode 16 "Memory Wipe" originally broadcast August 19, 2013
- Episode 17 "Avalanche!" originally broadcast September 16, 2013
- Episode 18 "Adam Up" originally broadcast September 23, 2013
- Episode 19 "Llama Drama" originally broadcast September 30, 2013
- Episode 20 "The Haunting of Mission Creek High" originally broadcast October 14, 2013
- Episode 21 "Perry 2.0" originally broadcast November 11, 2013
- Episode 22 "My Little Brother" originally broadcast November 18, 2013
- Episode 23 "Prank You Very Much" originally broadcast November 25, 2013
- Episode 24 "'Twas the Mission Before Christmas" originally broadcast December 2, 2013
- Episode 25 "Trent Gets Schooled" originally broadcast January 6, 2014
- Episode 26 "No Going Back" originally broadcast January 13, 2014

- Season 3

  - Episode 1 "Sink or Swim: Part One" originally broadcast February 17, 2014
  - Episode 2 "Sink or Swim: Part Two" originally broadcast February 17, 2014
  - Episode 3 "The Jet Wing" originally broadcast February 24, 2014
  - Episode 4 "Mission: Mission Creek High" originally broadcast March 3, 2014
  - Episode 5 "Zip It" originally broadcast March 10, 2014
  - Episode 6 "Not So Smart Phone" originally broadcast March 24, 2014
  - Episode 7 "Scramble the Orbs" originally broadcast April 7, 2014

- Episode 8 "Principal from Another Planet" originally broadcast April 14, 2014
- Episode 9 "Taken" originally broadcast April 21, 2014
- Episode 10 "Three Minus Bree" originally broadcast June 30, 2014
- Episode 11 "Which Father Knows Best?" originally broadcast July 7, 2014
- Episode 12 "Cyborg Shark Attack" originally broadcast July 18, 2014
- Episode 13 "You Posted What!?!: Part One" originally broadcast July 28, 2014
- Episode 14 "You Posted What!?!: Part Two" originally broadcast July 28, 2014
- Episode 15 "Armed and Dangerous" originally broadcast September 29, 2014
- Episode 16 "Alien Gladiators" originally broadcast October 13, 2014
- Episode 17 "Brother Battle" originally broadcast October 20, 2014
- Episode 18 "Spike Fright" originally broadcast October 24, 2014
- Episode 19 "Face-Off" originally broadcast November 10, 2014
- Episode 20 "Merry Glitchmas" originally broadcast December 1, 2014
- Episode 21 "Rise of the Secret Soldiers" originally broadcast January 26, 2015
- Episode 22 "Rise of the Secrets Soldiers" originally broadcast January 26, 2015
- Episode 23 "Bionic House Party" originally broadcast February 2, 2015
- Episode 24 "First Day of Bionic Academy" originally broadcast February 3, 2015
- Episode 25 "Adam Steps Up" originally broadcast February 4, 2015
- Episode 26 "Unauthorized Mission" originally broadcast February 5, 2015

- Season 4

  - Episode 1 "Bionic Rebellion" originally broadcast March 18, 2015
  - Episode 2 "Bionic Rebellion" originally broadcast March 18, 2015
  - Episode 3 "Left Behind" originally broadcast March 25, 2015
  - Episode 4 "Under Siege" originally broadcast April 1, 2015

- Episode 5 "Bionic Dog" originally broadcast April 8, 2015
- Episode 6 "Mission Mania" originally broadcast April 15, 2015
- Episode 7 "Simulation Manipulation" originally broadcast April 22, 2015
- Episode 8 "Forbidden Hero" originally broadcast July 1, 2015
- Episode 9 "Spider Island" originally broadcast July 8, 2015
- Episode 10 "Spike vs. Spikette" originally broadcast July 15, 2015
- Episode 11 "Space Elevator" originally broadcast July 29, 2015
- Episode 12 "Bionic Action Hero" originally broadcast August 5, 2015
- Episode 13 "Bionic Action Hero" originally broadcast August 5, 2015
- Episode 14 "One of Us" originally broadcast August 12, 2015
- Episode 15 "Mighty Med vs Lab Rats" originally broadcast July 22, 2015
- Episode 16 "Bob Zombie" originally broadcast September 30, 2015
- Episode 17 "Human Eddy" originally broadcast October 14, 2015
- Episode 18 "The Curse of the Screaming Skull" originally broadcast October 21, 2015
- Episode 19 "Lab Rats: On the Edge" originally broadcast November 11, 2015
- Episode 20 "Lab Rats: On the Edge" originally broadcast November 11, 2015
- Episode 21 "Ultimate Tailgate Challenge" originally broadcast December 2, 2015
- Episode 22 "And Then There Were Four" originally broadcast January 13, 2016
- Episode 23 "Space Colony: Part One" originally broadcast January 20, 2016
- Episode 24 "Space Colony: Part Two" originally broadcast January 20, 2016
- Episode 25 "The Vanishing: Part 1" originally broadcast February 3, 2016
- Episode 26 "The Vanishing: Part 2" originally broadcast February 3, 2016

Mighty Med

Originally Broadcast on Disney XD
Streaming on Disney+

- Creators
    - Jim Bernstein
    - Andy Schwartz
- Production Company
    - Disney Channel
    - It's a Laugh Productions
- Main Cast (in credited order)
    - Bradley Steven Perry as Kaz
    - Jake Short as Oliver
    - Paris Berelc as Skylar Storm
    - Devan Leos as Alan Dias
    - Carlos Lacamara as Dr. Horace Diaz
    - Jamie Denbo as Bridget
- Episode Names and Original Broadcast Dates
    - Season 1
        - Episode 1 "Saving the People Who Save People (Part 1)" originally broadcast October 7, 2013
        - Episode 2 "Saving the People Who Save People (Part 2)" originally broadcast October 7, 2013
        - Episode 3 "Frighty Med" originally broadcast October 14, 2013
        - Episode 4 "I, Normo" originally broadcast October 21, 2013
        - Episode 5 "Sm'oliver's Travels" originally broadcast October 28, 2013
        - Episode 6 "Pranks for Nothing" originally broadcast November 4, 2013
        - Episode 7 "It's Not the End of the World" originally broadcast November 11, 2013
        - Episode 8 "Evil Gus" originally broadcast January 13, 2014
        - Episode 9 "Alan's Reign of Terror" originally broadcast February 3, 2014
        - Episode 10 "So You Think You Can Be a Sidekick" originally broadcast February 10, 2014
        - Episode 11 "Lockdown" originally broadcast February 24, 2014
        - Episode 12 "All That Kaz" originally broadcast March 10, 2014
        - Episode 13 "The Friend of My Friend Is My Enemy" originally broadcast March 24, 2014
        - Episode 14 "Atomic Blast from the Past" originally broadcast March 31, 2014
        - Episode 15 "Growing Pains" originally broadcast April 7, 2014

  - Episode 16 "Night of the Living Nightmare" originally broadcast April 14, 2014
  - Episode 17 "Mighty Mad" originally broadcast April 21, 2014
  - Episode 18 "Fantasy League of Heroes" originally broadcast June 9, 2014
  - Episode 19 "Copy Kaz" originally broadcast June 16, 2014
  - Episode 20 "Guitar Superhero" originally broadcast June 23, 2014
  - Episode 21 "Free Wi-Fi" originally broadcast June 30, 2014
  - Episode 22 "Two Writers Make a Wrong" originally broadcast July 7, 2014
  - Episode 23 "Are You Afraid of the Shark?" originally broadcast July 18, 2014
  - Episode 24 "The Pen Is Mighty Med-ier Than the Sword" originally broadcast July 21, 2014
  - Episode 25 "There's a Storm Coming (Part 1)" originally broadcast September 15, 2014
  - Episode 26 "There's a Storm Coming (Part 2)" originally broadcast September 15, 2014

- Season 2

  - Episode 1 "How the Mighty Med Have Fallen" (Part 1) originally broadcast October 20, 2014
  - Episode 2 "How the Mighty Med Have Fallen" (Part 2) originally broadcast October 24, 2014
  - Episode 3 "Lair, Lair" originally broadcast November 3, 2014
  - Episode 4 "Mighty Mole" originally broadcast November 10, 2014
  - Episode 5 "The Claw Prank Redemption" originally broadcast December 1, 2014
  - Episode 6 "Do You Want to Build a Lava-Man?" originally broadcast January 5, 2015
  - Episode 7 "Storm's End" originally broadcast January 12, 2015
  - Episode 8 "Future Tense" originally broadcast March 4, 2015
  - Episode 9 "Stop Bugging Me" originally broadcast March 11, 2015
  - Episode 10 "Less than Hero" originally broadcast March 25, 2015
  - Episode 11 "Oliver Hatches the Eggs" originally broadcast April 1, 2015
  - Episode 12 "Sparks Fly" originally broadcast April 7, 2015
  - Episode 13 "Wallace and Clyde: A Grand Day Out" originally broadcast April 15, 2015

        - Episode 14 "The Key to Being a Hero" originally broadcast July 1, 2015
        - Episode 15 "New Kids Are the Docs" originally broadcast July 8, 2015
        - Episode 16 "It's a Matter of Principal" originally broadcast July 15, 2015
        - Episode 17 "Living the Dream" originally broadcast July 22, 2015
        - Episode 18 "Lab Rats vs. Mighty Med" originally broadcast August 12, 2015
        - Episode 19 "Thanks for the Memory Drives" originally broadcast August 19, 2015
        - Episode 20 "The Dirt on Kaz & Skylar" originally broadcast November 6, 2015
        - Episode 21 "The Mother of All Villains" originally broadcast November 6, 2015

The Thundermans

Originally broadcast on Nickelodeon
Streaming on Paramount+

- Creator
    - Jed Springarn
- Production Company
    - Nickelodeon Productions
    - Uptown Productions
- Main Cast (in credited order)
    - Kira Kosarin as Phoebe Thunderman
    - Jack Griffo as Max Thunderman
    - Addison Riecke as Nora Thunderman
    - Diego Velazquez as Billy Thunderman
    - Chris Tallman as Hank Thunderman
    - Rosa Blasi as Barb Thunderman
    - Dana Snyder as Dr. Colosso
    - Maya Le Clark as Chloe Thunderman
    - Audrey Whitby as Cherry Seinfeld
    - Ryan Whitney as Allison
- Episode Names and Original Broadcast Dates
    - Season 1

- Episode 1 "Adventures in Supersitting" originally broadcast October 14, 2013
- Episode 2 "Phoebe vs. Max" originally broadcast November 2, 2013
- Episode 3 "Dinner Party" originally broadcast November 9, 2013
- Episode 4 "Report Card" originally broadcast November 16, 2013
- Episode 5 "Ditch Day" originally broadcast November 23, 2013
- Episode 6 "This Looks Like a Job For..." originally broadcast November 30, 2013
- Episode 7 "Weekend Guest" originally broadcast December 7, 2013
- Episode 8 "You Stole My Thunder, Man" originally broadcast December 7, 2013
- Episode 9 "Weird Science Fair" originally broadcast January 4, 2014
- Episode 10 "Crime After Crime" originally broadcast January 11, 2014
- Episode 11 "Going Wonkers" originally broadcast February 8, 2014
- Episode 12 "Restaurant Crashers" originally broadcast February 15, 2014
- Episode 13 "Thundersense" originally broadcast March 15, 2014
- Episode 14 "Phoebe's a Clone Now" originally broadcast March 15, 2014
- Episode 15 "Have an Ice Birthday" originally broadcast March 22, 2014
- Episode 16 "Nothing to Lose Sleepover" originally broadcast April 26, 2014
- Episode 17 "Pretty Little Choirs" originally broadcast May 3, 2014
- Episode 18 "Paging Dr. Thunderman" originally broadcast May 3, 2014
- Episode 19 "Up, Up, and Vacay!" originally broadcast May 31, 2014
- Episode 20 "Breaking Dad" originally broadcast June 14, 2014

- Season 2
  - Episode 1 "Thunder Van" originally broadcast September 13, 2014
  - Episode 2 "Four Supes and a Baby" originally broadcast September 20, 2014
  - Episode 3 "Max's Minions" originally broadcast September 27, 2014

- Episode 4 "Pheebs Will Rock You" originally broadcast October 4, 2014
- Episode 5 "The Haunted Thundermans" originally broadcast October 11, 2014
- Episode 6 "Shred It Go" originally broadcast November 1, 2014
- Episode 7 "Blue Detective" originally broadcast November 8, 2014
- Episode 8 "Cheer and Present Danger" originally broadcast November 15, 2014
- Episode 9 "Change of Art" originally broadcast November 22, 2014
- Episode 10 "Winter Thunderland" originally broadcast November 29, 2014
- Episode 11 "Parents Just Don't Thunderstand" originally broadcast January 24, 2015
- Episode 12 "Meet the Evilmans" originally broadcast February 23, 2015
- Episode 13 "The Neverfriending Story" originally broadcast February 24, 2015
- Episode 14 "You've Got Fail" originally broadcast February 25, 2015
- Episode 15 "Doubles Trouble" originally broadcast February 26, 2015
- Episode 16 "Who's Your Mommy?" originally broadcast March 2, 2015
- Episode 17 "The Amazing Rat Race" originally broadcast March 3, 2015
- Episode 18 "Mall Time Crooks" originally broadcast March 4, 2015
- Episode 19 "It's Not What You Link" originally broadcast March 5, 2015
- Episode 20 "Cape Fear" originally broadcast March 9, 2015
- Episode 21 "Call of Lunch Duty" originally broadcast March 10, 2015
- Episode 22 "One Hit Thunder" originally broadcast March 11, 2015
- Episode 23 "The Girl with the Dragon Snafu" originally broadcast March 25, 2015
- Episode 24 "A Hero Is Born" originally broadcast March 28, 2015

- Season 3
  - Episode 1 "Phoebe vs. Max: The Sequel" originally broadcast June 27, 2015

- Episode 2 "On the Straight and Arrow" originally broadcast July 11, 2015
- Episode 3 "Why You Buggin'?" originally broadcast July 18, 2015
- Episode 4 "Exit Stage Theft" originally broadcast July 25, 2015
- Episode 5 "Are You Afraid of the Park?" originally broadcast September 30, 2015
- Episode 6 "Evil Never Sleeps" originally broadcast October 7, 2015
- Episode 7 "Doppel-Gamers" originally broadcast October 14, 2015
- Episode 8 "Floral Support" originally broadcast October 21, 2015
- Episode 9 "Patch Me If You Can" originally broadcast October 28, 2015
- Episode 10 "Give Me a Break-Up" originally broadcast November 4, 2015
- Episode 11 "No Country for Old Mentors" originally broadcast November 11, 2015
- Episode 12 "Date Expectations" originally broadcast November 18, 2015
- Episode 13 "He Got Game Night" originally broadcast February 13, 2016
- Episode 14 "Kiss Me Nate" originally broadcast April 2, 2016
- Episode 15 "Dog Day After-School" originally broadcast June 4, 2016
- Episode 16 "Original Prankster" originally broadcast June 11, 2016
- Episode 17 "Chutes and Splatters" originally broadcast June 25, 2016
- Episode 18 "I'm Gonna Forget You, Sucka" originally broadcast July 9, 2016
- Episode 19 "Beat the Parents" originally broadcast July 16, 2016
- Episode 20 "Can't Spy Me Love" originally broadcast July 23, 2016
- Episode 21 "Robin Hood: Prince of Pheebs" originally broadcast July 30, 2016
- Episode 22 "Aunt Misbehavin'" originally broadcast August 6, 2016
- Episode 23 "Stealing Home" originally broadcast August 13, 2016
- Episode 24 "Back to School" originally broadcast August 13, 2016
- Episode 25 "Thundermans: Secret Revealed" originally broadcast October 10, 2016

- Season 4
    - Episode 1 "Happy Heroween" originally broadcast October 22, 2016
    - Episode 2 "Thundermans: Banished!" originally broadcast November 19, 2016
    - Episode 3 "Smells Like Team Spirit" originally broadcast January 7, 2017
    - Episode 4 "Max to the Future" originally broadcast January 14, 2017
    - Episode 5 "Better Off Wed" originally broadcast January 21, 2017
    - Episode 6 "Parks & T-Rex" originally broadcast January 28, 2017
    - Episode 7 "Date of Emergency" originally broadcast February 4, 2017
    - Episode 8 "Orange Is the New Max" originally broadcast February 18, 2017
    - Episode 9 "Ditch Perfect" originally broadcast February 25, 2017
    - Episode 10 "May Z-Force Be with You" originally broadcast March 4, 2017
    - Episode 11 "21 Dump Street" originally broadcast June 3, 2017
    - Episode 12 "Super Dupers" originally broadcast June 10, 2017
    - Episode 13 "Come What Mayhem" originally broadcast June 17, 2017
    - Episode 14 "Thunder in Paradise" originally broadcast June 24, 2017
    - Episode 15 "Save the Past Dance" originally broadcast November 18, 2017
    - Episode 16 "Z's All That" originally broadcast January 6, 2018
    - Episode 17 "Can't Hardly Date" originally broadcast January 13, 2018
    - Episode 18 "Revenge of the Smith" originally broadcast January 20, 2018
    - Episode 19 "Nowhere to Slide" originally broadcast January 27, 2018
    - Episode 20 "Significant Brother" originally broadcast February 3, 2018
    - Episode 21 "Rhythm n' Shoes" originally broadcast February 17, 2018
    - Episode 22 "Make It Pop Pop" originally broadcast February 24, 2018
    - Episode 23 "Side-Kicking and Screaming" originally broadcast March 3, 2018

        - Episode 24 "Cookie Mistake" originally broadcast March 10, 2018
        - Episode 25 "All the President's Thunder-Men" originally broadcast March 17, 2018
        - Episode 26 "Mad Max: Beyond Thunderhome" originally broadcast May 25, 2018
        - Episode 27 "The Thundredth" originally broadcast May 25, 2018
        - Episode 28 "Looperheroes" originally broadcast May 25, 2018

Henry Danger

Originally broadcast on Nickelodeon
Streaming on Paramount+

- Creators
    - Dana Olsen
    - Dan Schneider
- Production Company
    - Schneider's Bakery
    - Uptown Productions
- Main Cast (in credited order)
    - Jace Norman as Henry Hart/Kid Danger
    - Cooper Barnes as Ray Manchester/Captain Man
    - Riele Downs as Charlotte Page
    - Sean Ryan Fox as Jasper Dunlop
    - Ella Anderson as Piper Hart
    - Michael D. Cohen as Schwoz
    - Jeffrey Nicholas Brown as Jake Hart
    - Kelly Sullivan as Kris Hart
- Episode Names and Original Broadcast Dates
    - Season 1
        - Episode 1 "The Danger Begins: Part One" originally broadcast July 26, 2014
        - Episode 2 "The Danger Begins: Part Two" originally broadcast July 26, 2014
        - Episode 3 "Mo' Danger, Mo' Problems" originally broadcast September 13, 2014
        - Episode 4 "The Secret Gets Out" originally broadcast September 20, 2014
        - Episode 5 "Tears of the Jolly Beetle" originally broadcast September 27, 2014

- Episode 6 "Substitute Teacher" originally broadcast October 4, 2014
- Episode 7 "Jasper Danger" originally broadcast October 18, 2014
- Episode 8 "The Space Rock" originally broadcast November 1, 2014
- Episode 9 "Birthday Girl Down" originally broadcast November 8, 2014
- Episode 10 "Too Much Game" originally broadcast November 15, 2014
- Episode 11 "Henry the Man-Beast" originally broadcast November 22, 2014
- Episode 12 "Invisible Brad" originally broadcast January 10, 2015
- Episode 13 "Spoiler Alert" originally broadcast January 24, 2015
- Episode 14 "Let's Make a Steal" originally broadcast January 31, 2015
- Episode 15 "Super Volcano" originally broadcast February 7, 2015
- Episode 16 "My Phony Valentine" originally broadcast February 14, 2015
- Episode 17 "Caved In" originally broadcast February 28, 2015
- Episode 18 "Elevator Kiss" originally broadcast March 7, 2015
- Episode 19 "Man of the House" originally broadcast March 14, 2015
- Episode 20 "Dream Busters" originally broadcast March 21, 2015
- Episode 21 "Kid Grounded" originally broadcast April 4, 2015
- Episode 22 "Captain Jerk" originally broadcast April 11, 2015
- Episode 23 "The Bucket Trap" originally broadcast April 18, 2015
- Episode 24 "Henry & the Bad Girl, Part 1" originally broadcast May 2, 2015
- Episode 25 "Henry & the Bad Girl, Part 2" originally broadcast May 9, 2015
- Episode 26 "Jasper's Real Girlfriend" originally broadcast May 16, 2015

- Season 2
    - Episode 1 "The Beat Goes On" originally broadcast September 12, 2015
    - Episode 2 "One Henry, Three Girls: Part 1" originally broadcast September 19, 2015

    - Episode 3 "One Henry, Three Girls: Part 2" originally broadcast September 26, 2015
    - Episode 4 "Henry & the Woodpeckers" originally broadcast October 3, 2015
    - Episode 5 "Captain Man Goes on Vacation" originally broadcast October 10, 2015
    - Episode 6 "The Time Jerker" originally broadcast November 7, 2015
    - Episode 7 "Secret Beef" originally broadcast November 14, 2015
    - Episode 8 "Henry's Jelly" originally broadcast November 21, 2015
    - Episode 9 "Christmas Danger" originally broadcast November 28, 2015
    - Episode 10 "Indestructible Henry, Part 1" originally broadcast March 19, 2016
    - Episode 11 "Indestructible Henry, Part 2" originally broadcast March 26, 2016
    - Episode 12 "Text, Lies & Video" originally broadcast April 9, 2016
    - Episode 13 "Opposite Universe" originally broadcast April 16, 2016
    - Episode 14 "Grave Danger" originally broadcast April 23, 2016
    - Episode 15 "Ox Pox" originally broadcast April 30, 2016
    - Episode 16 "Twin Henrys" originally broadcast May 7, 2016
    - Episode 17 "Danger & Thunder" originally broadcast June 18, 2016
    - Episode 18 "I Know Your Secret" originally broadcast July 17, 2016

  - Season 3

    - Episode 1 "A Fiñata Full of Death Bugs" originally broadcast September 17, 2016
    - Episode 2 "Love Muffin" originally broadcast September 24, 2016
    - Episode 3 "Scream Machine" originally broadcast October 1, 2016
    - Episode 4 "Mouth Candy" originally broadcast October 8, 2016
    - Episode 5 "The Trouble with Frittles" originally broadcast November 5, 2016
    - Episode 6 "Hour of Power" originally broadcast November 11, 2016
    - Episode 7 "Dodging Danger" originally broadcast December 3, 2016

   - Episode 8 "Double Date Danger" originally broadcast February 11, 2017
   - Episode 9 "Space Invaders, Part 1" originally broadcast March 11, 2017
   - Episode 10 "Space Invaders, Part 2" originally broadcast March 18, 2017
   - Episode 11 "Gas or Fail" originally broadcast March 25, 2017
   - Episode 12 "JAM Session" originally broadcast April 8, 2017
   - Episode 13 "License to Fly" originally broadcast April 15, 2017
   - Episode 14 "Green Fingers" originally broadcast April 22, 2017
   - Episode 15 "Stuck in Two Holes" originally broadcast April 29, 2017
   - Episode 16 "Live & Dangerous: Part 1" originally broadcast September 16, 2017
   - Episode 17 "Live & Dangerous: Part 2" originally broadcast September 23, 2017
   - Episode 18 "Balloons of Doom" originally broadcast September 30, 2017
   - Episode 19 "Swellview's Got Talent" originally broadcast October 7, 2017

- Season 4

   - Episode 1 "Sick & Wired" originally broadcast October 21, 2017
   - Episode 2 "Brawl in the Hall" originally broadcast November 4, 2017
   - Episode 3 "The Rock Box Dump" originally broadcast November 11, 2017
   - Episode 4 "Danger Games: Part One" originally broadcast November 25, 2017
   - Episode 5 "Danger Games: Part Two" originally broadcast November 25, 2017
   - Episode 6 "Danger Games: Part Three" originally broadcast November 25, 2017
   - Episode 7 "Toon in for Danger" originally broadcast January 15, 2018
   - Episode 8 "Meet Cute Crush" originally broadcast February 10, 2018
   - Episode 9 "Back to the Danger, Part 1" originally broadcast March 24, 2018
   - Episode 10 "Back to the Danger, Part 2" originally broadcast March 31, 2018
   - Episode 11 "Budget Cuts" originally broadcast April 7, 2018
   - Episode 12 "Diamonds Are for Heather" originally broadcast April 14, 2018

- Episode 13 "Car Trek" originally broadcast April 28, 2018
- Episode 14 "Toddler Invasion" originally broadcast May 5, 2018
- Episode 15 "Captain Man-kini" originally broadcast May 12, 2018
- Episode 16 "Saturday Night Lies" originally broadcast May 19, 2018
- Episode 17 "Henry's Frittle Problem" originally broadcast September 22, 2018
- Episode 18 "Spelling Bee Hard" originally broadcast September 29, 2018
- Episode 19 "Up the Stairs!" originally broadcast October 6, 2018
- Episode 20 "Danger Things" originally broadcast October 8, 2018
- Episode 21 "Rubber Duck" originally broadcast October 13, 2018
- Episode 22 "Flabber Gassed" originally broadcast October 20, 2018

- Season 5

  - Episode 1 "Henry's Birthday" originally broadcast November 3, 2018
  - Episode 2 "Whistlin' Susie" originally broadcast November 10, 2018
  - Episode 3 "Thumb War: Part One" originally broadcast November 17, 2018
  - Episode 4 "Thumb War: Part Two" originally broadcast November 17, 2018
  - Episode 5 "The Great Cactus Con" originally broadcast November 24, 2018
  - Episode 6 "Part 1: A New Evil" originally broadcast January 5, 2019
  - Episode 7 "Part 2: A New Darkness" originally broadcast January 12, 2019
  - Episode 8 "Part 3: A New Hero" originally broadcast January 19, 2019
  - Episode 9 "Broken Armed and Dangerous" originally broadcast January 26, 2019
  - Episode 10 "Knight & Danger" originally broadcast February 2, 2019
  - Episode 11 "Grand Theft Otto" originally broadcast February 16, 2019
  - Episode 12 "The Whole Bilsky Family" originally broadcast February 23, 2019

- Episode 13 "Secret Room" originally broadcast March 2, 2019
- Episode 14 "My Dinner with Bigfoot" originally broadcast March 9, 2019
- Episode 15 "Charlotte Gets Ghosted" originally broadcast March 16, 2019
- Episode 16 "I Dream of Danger" originally broadcast March 23, 2019
- Episode 17 "Holey Moley" originally broadcast June 15, 2019
- Episode 18 "Love Bytes" originally broadcast June 22, 2019
- Episode 19 "Double-O Danger" originally broadcast June 29, 2019
- Episode 20 "Massage Chair" originally broadcast July 13, 2019
- Episode 21 "Henry Danger: The Musical: Part One" originally broadcast July 27, 2019
- Episode 22 "Henry Danger: The Musical: Part Two" originally broadcast July 27, 2019
- Episode 23 "Sister Twister Part 1" originally broadcast September 21, 2019
- Episode 24 "Sister Twister Part 2" originally broadcast September 28, 2019
- Episode 25 "A Tale of Two Pipers" originally broadcast October 5, 2019
- Episode 26 "Story Tank" originally broadcast October 12, 2019
- Episode 27 "Captain Mom" originally broadcast November 2, 2019
- Episode 28 "Visible Brad" originally broadcast November 9, 2019
- Episode 29 "EnvyGram Wall" originally broadcast November 16, 2019
- Episode 30 "Holiday Punch" originally broadcast November 30, 2019
- Episode 31 "Mr. Nice Guy" originally broadcast January 11, 2020
- Episode 32 "Theranos Boot" originally broadcast January 18, 2020
- Episode 33 "Rumblr" originally broadcast January 25, 2020
- Episode 34 "Cave the Date" originally broadcast February 1, 2020
- Episode 35 "Escape Room" originally broadcast February 8, 2020
- Episode 36 "Game of Phones" originally broadcast February 15, 2020
- Episode 38 "Remember the Crimes" originally broadcast February 22, 2020

        - Episode 39 "The Beginning of the End" originally broadcast February 29, 2020
        - Episode 40 "Captain Drex" originally broadcast March 7, 2020
        - Episode 41 "The Fate of Danger: Part 1" originally broadcast March 14, 2020
        - Episode 42 "The Fate of Danger: Part 2" originally broadcast March 21, 2020

K.C. Undercover

Originally Broadcast on Disney Channel
Streaming on Disney+

- Creator
    - Corinne Marshall
- Production Company
    - Rob Lotterstein Productions
    - It's a Laugh Productions
- Main Cast (in credited order)
    - Zendaya as K.C. Cooper
    - Veronica Dunne as Marisa Clark
    - Kamil McFadden as Ernie Cooper
    - Trinitee as Judy Cooper
    - Tammy Townsend as Kira Cooper
    - Kadeem Hardison as Craig Cooper
    - Ross Butler as Brett Willis
    - Kara Royster as Abby Martin
    - Jasmine Guy as Erica Martin
    - Chris Tavarez as Darien
- Episode Names and Original Broadcast Dates
    - Season 1
        - Episode 1 "Pilot" originally broadcast January 15, 2015
        - Episode 2 "My Sister From Another Mother…Board" originally broadcast January 25, 2015
        - Episode 3 "Give Me a K! Give Me a C!" originally broadcast February 8, 2015
        - Episode 4 "Off the Grid" originally broadcast February 15, 2015
        - Episode 5 "Photo Bombed" originally broadcast March 1, 2015
        - Episode 6 "How K.C. Got Her Swag Back" originally broadcast March 8, 2015

- Episode 7 “Daddy’s Little Princess” originally broadcast March 29, 2015
- Episode 8 “Assignment: Get That Assignment” originally broadcast April 6, 2015
- Episode 9 “Spy-anoia Will Destroy Ya” originally broadcast April 19, 2015
- Episode 10 “Double Crossed: Part 1A” originally broadcast May 29, 2015
- Episode 11 “Double Crossed: Part 1B” originally broadcast May 29, 2015
- Episode 12 “Double Crossed: Part 2” originally broadcast May 30, 2015
- Episode 13 “Double Crossed: Part 3” originally broadcast May 31, 2015
- Episode 14 “The Stakeout Takeout” originally broadcast June 7, 2015
- Episode 15 “The Neighborhood Watchdogs” originally broadcast June 14, 2015
- Episode 16 “First Friend” originally broadcast June 26, 2015
- Episode 17 “Operation: The Other Side Part 1” originally broadcast July 12, 2015
- Episode 18 “Operation: The Other Side Part 2” originally broadcast July 19, 2015
- Episode 19 “K.C. and the Vanishing Lady” originally broadcast July 26, 2015
- Episode 20 “Debutante Baller” originally broadcast August 9, 2015
- Episode 21 “K.C.’s The Man” originally broadcast August 16, 2015
- Episode 22 “Runaway Robot Part 1” originally broadcast September 7, 2015
- Episode 23 “Runaway Robot Part 2” originally broadcast September 11, 2015
- Episode 24 “All Howl’s Eve” originally broadcast October 4, 2015
- Episode 25 “The Get Along Vault” originally broadcast October 18, 2015
- Episode 26 “Enemy of the State” originally broadcast November 8, 2015
- Episode 27 “’Twas the Fight Before Christmas” originally broadcast December 6, 2015
- Episode 28 “K.C. and Brett: The Final Chapter – Part 1” originally broadcast January 17, 2016
- Episode 29 “K.C. and Brett: The Final Chapter – Part 2” originally broadcast January 26, 2016

- Season 2
  - Episode 1 "Cooper's Reactivated! Part 1" originally broadcast March 6, 2016
  - Episode 2 "Cooper's Reactivated! Part 2" originally broadcast March 6, 2016
  - Episode 3 "Do You Want to Know a Secret" originally broadcast March 13, 2016
  - Episode 4 "Rebel With a Cuz" originally broadcast March 20, 2016
  - Episode 5 "The Mother of all Missions" originally broadcast April 10, 2016
  - Episode 6 "Accidents Will Happen" originally broadcast April 17, 2016
  - Episode 7 "Brainwashed" originally broadcast April 24, 2016
  - Episode 8 "The Truth Hurts" originally broadcast May 8, 2016
  - Episode 9 "Down in the Dumps" originally broadcast May 15, 2016
  - Episode 10 "Dance Like No One's Watching" originally broadcast May 22, 2016
  - Episode 11"The Love Jinx" originally broadcast June 16, 2016
  - Episode 12 "K.C. Levels Up" originally broadcast July 10, 2016
  - Episode 13 "Catch Him If You Can" originally broadcast July 17, 2016
  - Episode 14 "Sup, Dawg" originally broadcast July 24, 2016
  - Episode 15 "K.C. Undercover: Tightrope of Doom, Part One" originally broadcast August 7, 2016
  - Episode 16 "K.C. Undercover: Tightrope of Doom, Part Two" originally broadcast August 7, 2016
  - Episode 17 "The Legend of Bad, Bad Cleo Brown" originally broadcast August 14, 2016
  - Episode 18 "Spy of the Year Awards" originally broadcast September 11, 2016
  - Episode 19 "In Too Deep" originally broadcast September 18, 2016
  - Episode 20 "In Too Deep 2" originally broadcast September 25, 2016
  - Episode 21 "Virtual Insanity" originally broadcast October 2, 2016
  - Episode 22 "Undercover Mother" originally broadcast November 6, 2016
  - Episode 23 "Trust No One" originally broadcast November 13, 2016
  - Episode 24 "Holly Holly Not So Jolly" originally broadcast December 4, 2016

        - Episode 25 "Collision Course" originally broadcast January 6, 2017
        - Episode 26 "Family Feud" originally broadcast January 13, 2017

    - Season 3

        - Episode 1 "Coopers on the Run, Part 1" originally broadcast July 7, 2017
        - Episode 2 "Coopers on the Run, Part 2" originally broadcast July 7, 2017
        - Episode 3 "Welcome to the Jungle" originally broadcast July 14, 2017
        - Episode 4 "Out of the Water and Into the Fire" originally broadcast July 14, 2017
        - Episode 5 "Web of Lies" originally broadcast July 28, 2017
        - Episode 6 "Teen Drama" originally broadcast August 4, 2107
        - Episode 7 "K.C. Under Construction" originally broadcast August 11, 2017
        - Episode 8 "The Storm Maker" originally broadcast August 18, 2017
        - Episode 9 "Keep on Truckin'" originally broadcast August 25, 2017
        - Episode 10 "Unmasking the Enemy" originally broadcast November 3, 2017
        - Episode 11 "The Truth Will Set You Free" originally broadcast November 10, 2017
        - Episode 12 "Stormy Weather" originally broadcast November 17, 2017
        - Episode 13 "Deleted!" originally broadcast November 24, 2017
        - Episode 14 "Second Chances" originally broadcast January 15, 2018
        - Episode 15 "Revenge of the Van People" originally broadcast January 16, 2018
        - Episode 16 "The Gammy Files" originally broadcast January 17, 2018
        - Episode 17 "Take Me Out" originally broadcast January 18, 2018
        - Episode 18 "Twin it to Win It" originally broadcast January 22, 2018
        - Episode 19 "Cassandra Undercover" originally broadcast January 23, 2018
        - Episode 20 "K.C. Times Three" originally broadcast January 24, 2018

        - Episode 21 "The Domino Effect" originally broadcast January 29, 2018
        - Episode 22 "Domino 2: Barbecued" originally broadcast January 30, 2018
        - Episode 23 "Domino 3: Buggin' Out" originally broadcast January 31, 2018
        - Episode 24 "Domino 4: The Mask" originally broadcast February 1, 2018
        - Episode 25 "K.C. Undercover: The Final Chapter, Part 1" originally broadcast February 2, 2018
        - Episode 26 "K.C. Undercover: The Final Chapter, Part 2" originally broadcast February 2, 2018

Lab Rats: Elite Force

Originally Broadcast on Disney XD
Streaming on Disney+

- Creators
    - Bryan Moore
    - Chris Peterson
- Production Company
    - BriteLite Productions
    - It's a Laugh Productions
- Main Cast (in credited order)
    - William Brent as Chase Davenport
    - Bradley Steven Perry as Kax
    - Jake Short as Oliver
    - Paris Berelc as Skylar Storm
    - Kelli Berglund as Bree Davenport
    - Maile Flanagan as Perry
    - Jeremy Kent Jackson as Douglas Davenport
    - Hal Sparks as Donald Davenport
- Episode Names and Original Broadcast Dates
    - Season 1
        - Episode 1 "The Rise of Five" originally broadcast March 2, 2016
        - Episode 2 "Holding Out for a Hero" originally broadcast March 9, 2016
        - Episode 3 "Power Play" originally broadcast March 16, 2016

        - Episode 4 "The Superhero Code" originally broadcast March 23, 2016
        - Episode 5 "Need for Speed" originally broadcast March 30, 2016
        - Episode 6 "Follow the Leader" originally broadcast April 6, 2016
        - Episode 7 "The List" originally broadcast April 13, 2016
        - Episode 8 "Coming Through in the Clutch" originally broadcast July 5, 2016
        - Episode 9 "The Intruder" originally broadcast September 10, 2016
        - Episode 10 "The Rock" originally broadcast September 17, 2016
        - Episode 11 "Home Sweet Home" originally broadcast September 24, 2016
        - Episode 12 "Home Sweet Home: Part 1" originally broadcast September 26, 2016
        - Episode 13 "Home Sweet Home: Part 2" originally broadcast September 27, 2016
        - Episode 14 "Shape Shifting" originally broadcast originally broadcast October 1, 2016
        - Episode 15 "Game of Drones" originally broadcast October 8, 2016
        - Episode 16 "They Grow Up So Fast" originally broadcast October 15, 2016
        - Episode 17 "The Attack" originally broadcast October 22, 2016

Ultra-Violet & Black Scorpion
Originally Broadcast on Disney Channel
Streaming on Disney+

- Creators
    - Leo Chu
    - Eric Garcia
    - Dan Hernandez
- Production Company
    - Chu Garcia
    - Chu Media
    - GWave Productions
    - Moxie 88
- Main Cast (in credited order)
    - Scarlet Estevez as Violet Rodriguez/Ultra-Violet

- J.R. Villarreal as Cruz de la Vega/Black Scorpoin
- Marianna Burelli as Nina Rodiguez
- Juan Alfonso as Juan Carlos Rodriguez
- Brandon Rossel as Santiago Rodriguez
- Zelia Ankrum as Maya Miller-Martinez
- Bryan Blanco as Luis Leon
- Lorena Jorge as Catalina/Cascada

- Episode Names and Original Broadcast Dates
  - Episode 1 "The Violet Behind the Mask" originally broadcast June 3, 2022
  - Episode 2 "You Like Me! You Really Like Me" originally broadcast June 3, 2022
  - Episode 3 "Lucha Royale" originally broadcast June 10, 2022
  - Episode 4 "Sleepover Showdown" originally broadcast June 17, 2022
  - Episode 5 "The Legend of the Twelve Masks" originally broadcast June 24, 2022
  - Episode 6 "Chisme!Chisme! Read All About It!" originally broadcast July 1, 2022
  - Episode 7 "Ultra Matchmaker" originally broadcast July 8, 2022
  - Episode 8 "Ultra-Violet Unmasked" originally broadcast July 15, 2022
  - Episode 9 "Cascada" originally broadcast July 22, 2022
  - Episode 10 "Lucha Rules!" originally broadcast July 29, 2022
  - Episode 11 "Ultra Friend, Ultra Flake" originally broadcast October 7, 2022
  - Episode 12 "Forgive Me Not" originally broadcast October 14, 2022
  - Episode 13 "Highkey Anxiety" originally broadcast October 22, 2022
  - Episode 14 "Luis Leon Won't Go Home" originally broadcast October 28, 2022
  - Episode 15 "Cape Night" originally broadcast November 4, 2022
  - Episode 16 "Ultra-Violet vs. Black Scorpion" originally broadcast November 11, 2022

The Villains of Valley View
Originally Broadcast on Disney Channel
Streaming on Disney+

- Creators
  - Bryan Moore
  - Chris Peterson

- Production Company
  - BriteLite Studio
  - Britelite Productions
  - Disney Branded Television
  - It's a Laugh Productions
  - Too Much Coffee
- Main Cast (in credited order)
  - Isabella Pappas as Amy/Havoc
  - Malachi Barton as Colby/Flashform
  - Reed Horstmann as Jake/Chaos
  - Kaden Muller-Janssen as Hartley
  - Lucy Davis as Eva/Surge
  - James Patrick Stuart as Vic/Kraniac
  - Patricia Belcher as Celia
  - Mariah Iman Wilson as Starling
  - Steve Blum as Onyx
  - Kainalu Moya as Declan/Oculus
  - Giselle Torres as Gem
- Episode Names and Original Broadcast Dates
  - Season 1
    - Episode 1 "Finding Another Dimension" originally broadcast June 3, 2022
    - Episode 2 "Trust No One" originally broadcast June 3, 2022
    - Episode 3 "The Villain Experience" originally broadcast June 10, 2022
    - Episode 4 "Belts, Bulls & Superfans" originally broadcast June 17, 2022
    - Episode 5 "ColossaCon!" originally broadcast June 24, 2022
    - Episode 6 "Super Secrets" originally broadcast July 1, 2022
    - Episode 7 "A Little Havoc" originally broadcast July 8, 2022
    - Episode 8 "The Two Jakes" originally broadcast July 15, 2022
    - Episode 9 "Battle for My Brother" originally broadcast July 22, 2022
    - Episode 10 "Unleash the Chaos" originally broadcast July 29, 2022
    - Episode 11 "Havoc-ween" originally broadcast October 2, 2022
    - Episode 12 "Showdown at the Round Up" originally broadcast October 7, 2022
    - Episode 13 "Friend or Foe" originally broadcast October 14, 2022
    - Episode 14 "Vials and Tribulations" originally broadcast October 21, 2022

    - Episode 15 "A Superhero in Valley View" originally broadcast October 28, 2022
    - Episode 16 "We Don't Care" originally broadcast November 4, 2022
    - Episode 17 "Bad Energy" originally broadcast November 11, 2022
    - Episode 18 "No Escape" originally broadcast November 18, 2022
    - Episode 19 "How the Villains Stole Christmas" originally broadcast December 2, 2022

- Season 2

    - In production at the time of book production

Index

For Product Safety Concerns and Information please contact our EU
representative GPSR@taylorandfrancis.com
Taylor & Francis Verlag GmbH, Kaufingerstraße 24, 80331 München, Germany

www.ingramcontent.com/pod-product-compliance
Lightning Source LLC
Chambersburg PA
CBHW070617310726
48982CB00001B/110
9781032972695